THE
MOTHER GARDEN

stories

Robin Romm

SCRIBNER

New York   London   Toronto   Sydney

SCRIBNER
1230 Avenue of the Americas
New York, NY 10020

SCRIBNER and design are trademarks of
Macmillan Library Reference USA, Inc., used under license
by Simon & Schuster, the publisher of this work.

For information about special discounts for bulk purchases,
please contact Simon & Schuster Special Sales:
1-800-456-6798 or business@simonandschuster.com

Designed by Kyoko Watanabe
Text set in Granjon

Manufactured in the United States of America

1   3   5   7   9   10   8   6   4   2

Library of Congress Cataloging-in-Publication Data

Romm, Robin.
The mother garden : stories / Robin Romm.
p.   cm.
1. Loss (Psychology)—Fiction. I. Title.

PS3618.O654M68 2007
813'.6—dc22   2007061711

ISBN-13: 978-1-4165-3902-5
ISBN-10: 1-4165-3902-6

Many of the stories in this collection have appeared elsewhere,
in slightly different form: "No Small Feat" in *Tin House*; "Lost
and Found" in *The Threepenny Review*; "Where Nothing Is" in
Cimarron Review; "The Arrival" in *One Story*; "A Romance" in
Northwest Review; and "Celia's Fish" in *Quarterly West*.

for my mother, Jacquelyn

Is one of the symptoms loss of faith?

Or faith in loss?

— AMY HEMPEL

Contents

THE
MOTHER GARDEN

THE ARRIVAL

MY MOTHER'S GOING TO DIE. THIS IS FACT. AND there are things that must be done. Last week she instructed us to donate her retirement savings. My father hedged and I cried, but she remained firm. "These sorts of things shouldn't be left to the last minute," she said. She wanted to know where that money would end up, and she was too tired to make the calls herself. We diligently obliged, taking notes until we'd compiled an exhaustive array of possibilities. Now she's furious. After glancing at the list, she's decided we're ready to bury her.

"It's too much reality for me," she says. When she cries, the oxygen tubes get clogged and she has to pull them out. Then she can't breathe. My father's gone out for a walk, as he always does right before she breaks down. I'm left watching the ocean out the window, trying to arrange the problems into something we can talk about.

"We don't have to do this now," I say. (Or ever. You were the one who sent us on this absurd mission.) I want her to look strong, to stand up and start putting the dishes away.

My mother shakes her head.

"I don't want to die," she says. She's been wearing the same blue fleece zipper robe for days. She pulls a Kleenex from the box, yanks the tubes, and looks like she's strangling. I stand dumbly next to her, staring at the top of her head.

I've been visiting my parents at their beach cabin all week. It's warm for early spring. I can sit on the deck without a jacket and watch the waves hit rocks. Sometimes flocks of birds land on the craggy outcroppings. Sometimes a fishing boat appears on the horizon.

The cabin rests on a bluff outside Yachats, a small Oregon beach town. The few neighbors keep their distance, not knowing what to say to a hairless woman who puts an oxygen canister in the seat of her wheelchair, tottering alongside it, tubes pulsing and hissing. A new house is being built up the road; someday soon the dune grass will be filled with houses. They'll obscure the ocean view. Families will park cars on sparkling cement; kids will scatter toys on new lawns. But now there's only sky and sea and a handful of graying wood cabins. Crab nets hang from porches. Driftwood mobiles clatter in the wind. If you jump down the rocks, you are almost always alone with the crash of waves, the cry of gulls, the hard ridges of sand under your feet.

"Do you want some lunch?" I ask my mother. She's calmed down a bit, her eyes focused on the bright lights of the television. Lately, when she sits in the chair, staring at the screen, she looks childlike—it's in the downward pull of her bottom lip, the way her cheeks have puffed out from steroids.

"No thanks," she says. I root around the fridge and find

a large container of yogurt. From the deck, I see my father and the dogs walking back to the cabin. His bad knee makes his gait recognizable from a distance. Rhythmic and slow, he veers perpetually left. He's taken to wearing a news cap, like an old man.

A few minutes later, the dogs, Pico and Lila, bound up the stairs. They wag and drool, slide around the wood floors. My mother ignores them. My father lopes up, sets his coat on the banister, and goes into the bedroom. He'll take a nap now. And the dogs will calm down and follow him. And my mother will block out the world. And I will stare at my feet and feel so quiet it could be a spell that was cast over me.

Yesterday the three of us were sitting quietly on the deck, trying to feel the sun through the wind. No one spoke. My mother closed her eyes. My father gazed at the water. I noted how the deck wasn't made of real wood; it was a weird synthetic wood, gray like all the real wood on the rest of the house, not brown like the wood would have been when the house was new. And I wondered whether the deck was an add-on, built to match the gray wood, or whether at one point the brown house stood on the grass with a gray deck attached like a prosthetic limb. Then my father shot up, his spine a dart. "A whale!" he cried, delighted or distressed, it was hard to tell; he pointed at the blue-black expanse.

My mother nodded vigorously as I squinted out into the blueness. "Look at the roof to the right," she said, pointing her manicured nail toward the vastness. "Then look straight out." I couldn't see it.

It was just the spouting they saw; water in the distance emerging from more water in the distance, but it seemed to make them cheerful for a while. Now, sitting here on the deck with my bowl of yogurt, I think I see something moving. It could be a small log straying from one of the mills up the coast. It could be a large piece of foam. Maybe it's a sea lion?

"Hey!" I call into the house. "There's something in the water!" My mother turns. "Maybe a little whale?" I want it to be a whale. Please God, I know you don't like us, but if you're listening, let it be a whale—

"Really?" My mother hoists herself up and tugs at the tubing. She lumbers over to the deck. I point straight ahead.

My parents' bedroom window looks over the opposite side of the deck, and my father, unwilling to miss large life events like this, appears at the screen door with his binoculars.

"Where?" he says. We sit in silence. And then, close to the shore, the thing bobs again. This time it's gangly, struggling. It's not a whale.

"Oh God," I say. My father sets his binoculars down.

The person glides on a wave and crawls onto shore, collapsing a few feet from the tide line.

"Go down there," my mother says. "David, go see what's going on." My father adjusts his binoculars and puts them back up to his face.

"It's a woman," he says.

"Well, go down and see if she needs help!"

My father grips the railing.

"I'll go," I say.

A strong breeze blows the brownish grass toward the

water, making it look silver. Despite the proximity of the beach, it's hard to get to the sand from here. Steep, sharp rocks jut from the bluff.

The woman is sprawled facedown on the sand, palms open, her blond hair darkened by the water. She wears dirty white capri pants and a pink sweater.

"Hey!" I call from the top of the rocks. My father approaches. Without his hat, his bald spot shines in the sun. I squat, dangle one leg toward the beach, and jump. My father stays firmly planted on the grass above.

She's about my age, late twenties, early thirties and pretty, with freckles across her tanned face. A thick silver bracelet peeks from the ripped sleeve of her sweater. She's missing one shoe; the toenails on her bare foot shimmer with purple polish.

"What's happening?" my father calls.

"Nothing," I yell back. She twitches slightly, props herself up on an elbow, and jerks her head like she has water in her ear. A trickle runs from her nose, gets caught right above her curvy lips.

"Hey!" my father yells. We turn to look at him. He waves.

I take a tissue out of my pocket and hold it out to her. She grabs her curls, wrings them out.

"What the hell," she says, looking down at her body.

"Go get a towel," I call up to my father. He stands there for a moment like he wants to say something, then he turns, glancing back over his shoulder, and veers left toward the house.

She shakes her head, turns away from me, and looks into the sky. Mist rolls slowly in off the ocean, bringing with it a slow, cold wind. She moves uncomfortably for a moment, writhing in her skin. Then she grabs the sleeves of her sweater and yanks it over her head. She holds it away from her, twists the water out, and sets it neatly beside her on the sand. Her sexy lace camisole matches the purple of her toenails.

"It would be nice of you to tell me what's going on here," she says. She's snarling slightly, giving me the same lip-of-disdain the blond chemo nurse always gives my mother, as if putting the needle in the port is going to damage her nails, as if no one in nursing school had warned her that for this particular job, you were going to have to *touch* the sick.

My father trots back with the towel.

"Here you go!" he calls, and tosses it down to us. It lands on the rocks a few feet away.

She glares at me, waiting.

"I have no idea what's going on," I say to her. It's one of the old brown dog towels from the garage and I'm embarrassed to give it to her. "Do you want to dry off?" She snatches the towel.

"Whatever," she says and pats at her hair. She looks at me as if *I've* just washed up on *her* beach. "Where's my other shoe?"

Her name is Gracie and she has no choice. She has to come back to the house. We have a shower, a phone. She can figure out what to do. She scrapes her foot on the rocky incline and then walks stiffly next to my father and me, across the prickly grass.

"Are you all right?" my father asks her, his voice grave.

"I'm fine," she says. It's a doorstop of a tone.

My mother stands by the top of the stairs, waiting. The oxygen hisses a little tune up her nose. Gracie looks at my mother and freezes. It's always difficult, this moment—watching strangers assess and absorb my mother's display of bodily decline.

Gracie drips water onto the wood floor.

"Mom, this is Gracie. Gracie, this is Ellen."

"Hello," Gracie says, taking the final few steps toward her. She's visibly uncomfortable, shivering, and I can see her reservation as she extends her hand. "Sorry to intrude."

My mother takes Gracie's hand in both of her own. "You look how I feel, dear," she says, smiling the bright smile my father and I haven't seen in months. Gracie smiles too. Her teeth are obviously capped.

"I'm putting up water for tea," my mother says, shuffling toward the stove. "Why don't you hop in the shower and Nina'll get you some dry clothes to put on." She doesn't look at me when she says this. "There are towels under the sink. And if you need to use the phone, go ahead. There's one in the bedroom."

Gracie disappears into the bathroom.

"What happened?" my mother whispers.

"I have no idea," I whisper back. "She wasn't exactly forthcoming. In fact, she's kind of bitchy."

My mother turns away from me. "For God's sake, Nina. I can't imagine you'd be Pollyanna if you were wet and cold. What do you expect?" I turn to my father for backup, but he's vanished back into the bedroom with the dogs.

My mother goes to the fridge and starts taking out sandwich food.

"I can do that," I say, reaching for the cucumber. She swings it away.

"Contrary to popular belief," she says, raising her eyebrows, "I'm not dead yet." Her oxygen tube gets caught on the stool by the bar. I unhook it. She yanks the slack toward her and gets out the peeler.

"Go get Gracie some clothes," she says again, whacking the cucumber with the blade.

I take the stairs slowly. Is this just jealousy? That I can't make my mother stand up for lunch? That she hasn't called me "dear" in ages? The water from the shower rumbles. Every time Gracie flips her hair up there, I can hear the slap of water against the floor.

It's been months since I've seen my mother animated. In the last months she'd turned dour and brooding, yelling at my father and me for our worried looks, our bad taste in movies, our overeager willingness to be quiet. Or worse, she'd sit at the table and stare at the newspaper. If you talked to her, she would pretend not to hear. She was made of granite, she was waiting us out.

I didn't pack much for this trip. I sit beside my suitcase and finger my red shirt. I should have taken a pair of ugly, paint-stained sweats. Some dirty socks. A turkey costume.

Back upstairs, I set the clothes on the kitchen bar.

"Go knock and give them to Gracie," my mother says. She's cutting a peeled cucumber for the cream cheese sandwiches and she looks different—a few inches taller, her neck straight, shoulders square.

I stand in front of the bathroom door. It's quiet in there. My knock sounds loud.

"Yes?" Gracie sings. "Come in!" I open the door. She turns toward me, wrapped in one of my mother's red luxury bath sheets. She runs my mother's wooden brush through her hair—my mother's brush? Where did she dig that out from? My mother's eye shadow and foundation are on the counter as well.

"Thanks," she says, plucking the clothes from my hands. She takes the door and, with a smile that's tight-lipped and all eyes, gently shuts me out.

Back in the kitchen, my mother sets the little sandwiches on her nicest platter. She's cut up oranges, placing them around the sandwiches like little sun rays. A cup of mint tea steams beside it, for Gracie.

"That's pretty," I say.

"Go set the table," she says.

I set out the plates, heavy silverware, tall striped glasses. A woman in my mother's support group made the place mats. They're laminated copies of pastel parrots. Gracie emerges looking like she's hatched from the center of a flower, an oversized Thumbelina. Her blond curls hang heavy, towel-dried into damp ringlets. Her lanky body does something new to my clothes. The pants hang on her, suggesting long, shapely legs. The shirt gathers where she's pushed up the sleeves. She glides to the table.

"That's so pretty," she exclaims, looking down at the sandwich platter. It is pretty. It looks like an edible mandala.

"Thanks, dear," my mother says. "David?" she calls. "Come for lunch."

We take our seats around the table. The windows behind it stretch from floor to ceiling, grimy from the salt in the air. Outside the ocean does its ocean thing. It's blue and constantly in motion, eating away at the rocks, grinding pink shells and green bottles into sand.

My father looks at the sandwiches and for a moment he seems puzzled. Then he maneuvers one off the platter so that the cucumber garnish falls into a hole.

"It's been such a lovely week," my mother says. The oxygen hisses, stops, and hisses.

My father says, "You can see clear out to China."

Gracie smiles, holding a sandwich up. "It's stunning here," she says. "You've got a great piece of property."

At first, when the cancer started, we broke down, we got angry, we denied it was happening. My mother spent thousands of dollars on new appliances. (How could she die if she had a Swedish washing machine to pay off?) When she went into her only remission, we pretended she'd never been sick. We ignored the past year. It was a bad year, misbehaving. But when the cancer returned months later, blooming like a weed in her chest, we started to fight. I nagged my mother about homeopathic cures, special diets that involved eating nothing but seeds. My father invented ways of staying out of the house. But now, eight years later, we're made of a bendable substance. We listen to friends who've never lost anyone tell us *it's all part of life's mysterious cycle*. Everyone dies, we repeat. This is nothing special, the way she sits all day, frozen in remorse and fear, how she winces with pain when you lean in to hug her. *Stop,* she says, the word made more from air than noise. These things are now as normal as tea in the afternoon, wind over the sea. We've gone from hoping for miracle cures to just hoping the sandwiches are good.

"These are good," I say. They are good. Salty and creamy with a nice, crisp snap when you bite into the cucumber.

"I love your nails," Gracie says, leaning over to inspect my mother's hands. My mother has kept up her biweekly manicure. "That color looks so good with your skin tone. You've got such pale skin, like a doll's."

"I have this woman in Eugene," my mother says. "She's a miracle."

When we're finished eating, my mother invites Gracie onto the deck. Gracie stacks some plates and hands them over to me. My mother slides open the door.

"Aren't you tired?" I ask her. It sounds like an accusation. Usually, after she sits upright for a while, she has to lie down and use the breathing machine in the bedroom.

"I'm fine, Nina," she says, putting her hand on Gracie's back as they step outside.

From the window above the sink, I can see my mother and Gracie. Gracie's hair blows sideways. My mother stands near the railing. She says something. Gracie laughs and puts her hand on my mother's shoulder.

Gracie hasn't even glanced at the phone. Doesn't anyone need to know that she just washed up from a foamy sea, that she's wearing a dying woman's blush in a house full of hissing tubes and battered green canisters?

My father sits on the sofa, reading the paper. Pico rests near his legs, Lila near the empty fireplace. I get on the floor and put my head on Lila's wiry chest. She lifts her head to glance at me, deeply exhausted, the white hairs around her nose spreading out toward her eyes. Then she puts her heavy head back down.

"What do you think the deal is with that Gracie character?" my dad says, putting the paper aside.

"I know," I say, rolling off the dog's chest. "Where'd she come from?"

"Isn't there a play about this?" my father asks. "She's going to fool us all into thinking she's one of us, then she's going to steal the dogs. Or the cars."

"Or something," I say. "Mom seems to like her."

"Yeah," he says, gazing at the lamp in the corner of the room. "She does, doesn't she?"

When my mother likes something, my father is amazed. He'll buy raspberry soda and she'll slink off to finish the bottle and he'll come into my room to report that she liked it! She liked it!

But maybe this is the right way to deal with the dying: She likes cream puffs? We'll bring her cream puffs. She wants to yell at us for renting another movie with a dying woman in it (it didn't say it on the box, we checked!), then yell away! It's her world; we're just hanging around, trying to keep it turning.

My father puts the newspaper down. Pico stares at him, his eyes little machines of want.

"Pico's so passionate," my father says, looking back at the dog. "I love Pico."

The glass door opens. My mother slowly moves over the threshold, Gracie behind her.

"I'm going to take the dogs out," my father says.

"I'm going to lie down for a bit," my mother says, making her way down the hallway. I follow her and shut the door. She sits on her big turquoise bed.

"Can you hook up the bipap?" she says, lifting the mask. Once she straps that monster on, she'll be unable to talk.

"How are you?" I ask. She hates being asked this. She's told me this over and over again. "I'm peachy keen!" she'll say. "Never better! Why? Do I look sick?"

"Fine," she says. "Tired."

"The sandwiches were good," I say. She fiddles with the dial of the bipap machine. "So what's the deal with Gracie?" I ask. My mother looks up at me, surprised. Her eyebrows are thin from the drugs and when she raises them, they get lost in the flesh of her forehead.

"She's a lovely girl," my mother says. "She grew up in Wisconsin. Her father's an orthodontist."

"So how'd she wind up here?" I ask.

My mother shrugs. "Switch the tubes for me." And in a fast pull-strap motion, she's got the mask secured. The little motor in the gray box begins to sing. I go to the compressor and pull the tubing in.

The house is silent. My grandmother's oil paintings of forests and sunsets line the stairwell to my bedroom.

"Oh!" says Gracie, putting down the porcelain box that sits by my bed. "I didn't hear you."

She looks guilty. My dad's right. We'll turn around to get the milk out of the fridge and off she'll go with the checkbooks, the credit cards, my mother's wedding ring.

"I was looking for my bracelet," she says.

"Well. It's not here," I say. "Maybe check the bathroom."

"Yeah, good idea." Gracie fidgets and begins to smooth the bedspread with the side of her hand. When she finishes that, she studies her fingers as if a secret scroll might be hidden in her nail bed. "Your mom's great," she says. "Such a fighter."

"Thanks," I say.

"My mom's dead," she says. Her eyes transform, full of tears.

"I'm sorry," I say, but it comes out made of rocks. She's wearing my earrings.

Gracie follows my gaze. Her hands fly to her ears.

"I'm sorry," she says, wincing. "I was just trying them on—they're very pretty."

"Hard to resist," I say. "Maybe it's not a good idea for you to stay here. Can we get you a room in town for the night?"

Gracie crumples sideways onto the bed. She's a real faucet now, getting mascara on my pale yellow pillows. I struggle to think of what words to toss in the silence that will open up between us, but I'm saved when she begins an energetic round of sobs. She sounds like a goose.

I feel my body go still. I don't care about Gracie, why she's here, what she wants. And I don't care about her mother. "How'd she die?" I ask. Gracie struggles to calm. She swipes at her nose and takes a big, slobbery breath. "She drowned," she says. "She left my father in Madison and was living in some women's colony near Junction City and something happened, I guess she went skinny-dipping in the river." She reaches over for a tissue—all our rooms have boxes of tissues now. Aside from a little snot and a smear of black beneath her eyes, she still looks good, like she's made out of velvet or suede, not skin. The salt from her tears makes her eyes an even more outlandish shade of green.

"They never found the body?" I ask. This is one of my fantasies, that we'll wake up one day and my mother will have vanished. There'll be no body, no clues. And instead of being nowhere, she'll be everywhere, in everything.

"No, it washed up downriver near a farm," Gracie says. "The police called us."

Everyone dies, I'm tempted to tell her. *It's all part of life's mysterious cycle.* She takes another tissue.

"There's whiskey upstairs," I tell her.

Both of us walk slowly, our bare feet soft on the wood. I pour two shots in the tall glasses.

"Ice?" I ask.

"No, neat," she says, holding out her hand.

I pluck the list of donation possibilities from beneath the fruit bowl, where it seems to have landed permanently, gathering smudges and grease stains. All over the margins, my father's boxy writing lists numbers, organizations, people who'd help administer grants. I fold it in half and toss it in the recycle box at the end of the bar.

We stare at the refrigerator. I want to ask what she did the moment she found out. Did she drive? Did she sink to the carpet and cry? But I look at her ears, still a faint pink from yanking the earrings out, I think of her drifting on the wave toward shore, and I don't ask.

My mother comes into the kitchen, arranging her tubes. The creases from the bipap mask make her face look even more childlike. She glances at Gracie and the delight from this afternoon is gone; in its place is a flat, drugged fog. Gracie presses herself nervously against the counter's edge.

"Can't sleep?" I ask. A lighthouse down the coast tosses silver-white beams over the water. They dive and quiver, then disappear. The refrigerator kicks into a low rumble. Gracie rubs her palms over her hips, then turns and reaches for another glass. She pours my mother a shot. I start to object. She's not supposed to drink.

Gracie holds up her glass. "To arriving," she says.

My mother holds up the amber liquid with those magenta nails and seems to see something in it.

LOST AND FOUND

THE FIRST IMAGE THAT COMES TO ME IS NOT THE ONE
I might expect—my father lying naked in the desert,
wrapped in nothing but a dirty sheet. Instead it's a moment
indistinguishable from so many moments: my father's
thick steak of a body standing in my dim living room, the
television blaring, his mind reeling, his life a set of cards
stamped in symbols known only to him.

But let me start at the beginning.

I was out walking the dog in the hot Arizona morning,
tumbleweeds and cacti punctuating the barren landscape.
I liked the emptiness of this particular road. No cars
whooshed by, no other dog walkers walked. I could wake
up, put on my shorts, and wander for miles without seeing
anyone. My dog trotted dutifully beside me, but he didn't
like to walk. I was the one who liked spending my mornings out here, the sun on our shoulders, the dusty desert air
in our ears.

The dog hadn't shown interest in chasing jackrabbits—
or anything, for that matter—in a number of years. I held

his leash loosely, looped over my thumb. The leash was just part of the ritual, not a means of establishing control. But the day it happened, the day we found him, the dog became bizarrely animated, tugging wildly and leading me off the gravel road, into the sand and sagebrush, whining and gulping. Surprised, I fumbled for control, lost it, and followed him partly out of curiosity, partly because my thumb had become painfully entangled in the leash.

We walked a short distance to a patch of scraggly desert brush and there he was, a full-grown man, curled like a fetus, lying naked on a sheet beneath the paltry shade of a damaged cactus. His eyes were closed in blissful delirium, his fists balled like a child's. He was humming faintly, starving, near death, and a note hung from his foot on a decaying piece of twine.

This is your father, the note read. *Do as you will.*

"My father!" I said to the dog. The dog looked up at me, sad and patient, and tugged back in the direction of the car. I wrapped my father as best I could in the sheet and dragged him behind us.

At home, the dog slept fitfully, twitching and snorting on the rug near the door. I rubbed ointment into my father's burned skin as he slept on the sofa. In his delirium he cooed and reached for my face. The touch of his hand was like the leg of a large dry insect.

For a while I sat on a chair, watching my father sleep. His eyes were set far apart in his face like a lizard's. Deep lines stamped his sweaty brow. His skin was burned, but the color beneath the burn was peach, nothing like my own olive skin.

As he slept, I began to grow nervous. That unblinking desert sky left no room for doubt; but here in my living room, dark clouds gathered. What does a person do with a found father? It's easy to lose a father. They get sick, they get old, they die, they abandon. But no one ever finds a father—or at least this sort of thing is infrequent. I had no books on the subject, no similarly situated friends to ask for advice.

Would I have to take care of him? Dress him in a blue uniform and send him up the street to the French Immersion School? Or would he awake with a profession? A lawyer, maybe. Maybe a dentist. It'd be nice if he were very wealthy.

I grew anxious for something to do. While he slept, I ran to the store to buy him something to drink. He seemed so parched and leathery, dried up like jerky in the hot desert sun. But what should I buy him? Seltzer? Beer? Juice? Milk? I couldn't decide. I bought every beverage in the beverage aisle. Apple juice to zinfandel. After all, it's not every day you find your father.

When I returned to the house, there he was, sitting upright, rubbing his eyes. Blue blue eyes the color of cornflowers.

"Father?" I set the bags down on the beat-up floor. He squinted at me, stretched his arms up into the air, extended his legs out in front of him so that his knees popped.

"Excuse me," he said, and tugged a blanket from the arm of the sofa. With it wrapped like a towel around him, he got up and found the bathroom.

I filled the kitchen with the beverage bottles. Lined them up on the counter by color. Wine and berry coolers. Orange and carrot juices. Coffee and root beer. The shower ran for quite a while.

"Can you find something for me to wear?" he called

from the bathroom. I paused, looked at the bottles sparkling in the light.

Under my bed, where I keep journals and old letters and sweaters that I never wear, I also keep the clothes that Duncan left tangled in the sheets of the bed. They were all I had left of Duncan, except for a slow-moving sadness. I probably should have tossed them, but I liked the way that Duncan smelled; the clothes were more potpourri than memorabilia. Two pairs of hospital scrub pants, one T-shirt with a faded monkey on the front, a pair of argyle socks with a hole in the toe, and one pair of plaid boxer shorts. I gathered the clothes and slipped them through a crack in the bathroom door.

He emerged freshened, head erect, dressed in the monkey T-shirt and scrubs.

"I feel like a new man," he said. "A new man indeed." I smiled at him, but he looked at his outfit instead.

"Would you like something to drink?" I asked.

"Actually," he said, "I'd love to go to a café. I'd like to get out and about."

"Do you want company?" I asked. I imagined the two of us, wide-eyed, drinking coffee out of heavy white mugs and talking all morning. We would clarify what the past twenty-six years—

"No," he said. "Don't you bother. I'm up for a solo tour."

The dog woke from where he was sleeping in the corner of the room and looked at me with ancient, patient eyes.

"All right," I said, trying to mask my hurt. "There's a lunch counter two blocks away." I drew him a map. He smiled and nodded. His dark, wet-looking eyelashes lent the only softness to his square face. I caught myself trying to memorize them—the black fringe around his corn-flower eyes. What if he never returned? Would I be able to explain what he looked like? He reached out for the map, gently tugged it from my hands.

"Do you think I can borrow a few bucks?" he asked. I handed him the bills in my wallet. He winked and walked out the door.

It took a long time to adjust to him. I took him shopping for new clothes. We had very different tastes and this proved troublesome. "It's *my* money," I insisted when he wanted the silk American-flag boxer shorts. He made short, snippy exhalations and then, "I'll pay you back."

He got a job changing oil at the garage down the street. No one there seemed to care if he came from Arizona aristocracy or a hole in the center of the earth. No one asked questions and no one expected answers. He brought home his meager salary and I turned my office into a bedroom for him.

We didn't talk much. At first, I didn't want to pry. Maybe I feared he'd leave if I asked difficult questions, or maybe I just feared what I'd find out. Soon we settled into the rhythms of cohabitation, and the questions I had at first dissolved into the tickings of daily life. He left for work in the early morning, before I woke. I'd hear him rattle things in the refrigerator, clank around in the silverware drawer. He returned in the late afternoons and tromped around, car grease on his chin, leaving dark oily footprints on my white tiled floor. Beer in hand, he'd head into the living room to watch television.

"Did you see this?" my father called from the sofa. I'd bought the sofa only months before and already it was beyond repair, the black smudges as deep as the batting.

"What?" I called from my computer in the kitchen.

"This show," he cried. "It's so crazy! They just torture these people while they have to answer questions and if they can answer the question anyway—"

"I don't care," I called back.

A tiny silence and then, "No need to be rude."

"*Who's* being rude?" I asked.

"Well, I think you are," he said.

I tried to type louder.

"Maybe I should try to win at a game show," he yelled.

I stopped typing. My computer was missing a pixel and a line bisected the screen.

"Did you hear me?" he asked.

"Yes," I called back. "Yes, I heard you but I'm trying to work."

"Well, excuuuuuuse me," he called.

Duncan never knew his father. This attracted us to each other at first. I could sit in the big bowl of loss inside of him, and then he could sit in mine. I knew nothing about my father, though, and Duncan knew everything about his.

Duncan's father was a psychotherapist who kept meticulous journals about his life. "Today," the journals read, "I woke and walked Mercy [the dog] through the neighborhood, thinking about the baby asleep at home." Each day was recorded carefully and revealed a boring pattern like the day before. Duncan read and reread the journals. He found them entrancing. To me, they were proof of how boring most people's lives are. To Duncan, they were the pieces of the puzzle, the clues to his father's suicide.

The journals had a lot to do with why Duncan and I

split up. I couldn't listen to him read them anymore. We went on a trip to northern California. I wanted to see the ocean, the way it would break on the cliffs and spatter up into the sky. Duncan wanted to sit on the cliffs and read his father's journals. "Today," he read, "after walking Mercy, I returned home to reread my notes about patient 106."

"Don't you ever get bored with that?" I asked. Duncan jutted his chin and raised his eyebrows. "No. I'm sorry if I'm boring *you*."

"It's just that we've read this part already."

"This is all I have left of him," Duncan said. "I think that should matter to you."

The waves crashed against the cliffs and sent foam into the sky but it didn't seem magical, like the image in my mind. Just water spraying up from the ocean and then falling back onto the rocks.

The truth is, it didn't really matter to me. The journals, Duncan's feeling of abandonment, the way he cried when we fought, as if I was dying. He used to reach for me when I was angry, his fingers pulling me toward him. He'd hold on to me as if I were a buoy and I would feel a little bit claustrophobic. I loved him, but I didn't really understand that sort of grief.

I never mourned the loss of my father. My mother didn't talk about him, and by the time I was old enough to confront her, she was dying. He was a forest fire that burned before I was born. I had no clues, no puzzle pieces to spend my life putting together. Just a clean, sharp hole. Duncan did not have this clarity; he lived amidst a dark bloody thing full of roots and broken teeth.

Eventually Duncan started spending a lot of time with a girl named Lucy whose parents had died in a car wreck when she was young. I felt Duncan drifting away and I couldn't stop him. I'm not even sure I wanted to stop him. I watched his eyes fill with distraction, muddy with small dishonesties that soon became large ones. And then, one day, he was gone.

I often wondered what it would have been like if Duncan and I were still together the day I found my father. Would it have given us hope—hope that our lives would be full of such unexpected fortune? Would he have been jealous? Or would he have seen impending gloom hanging low on the horizon?

But even if Duncan could have detected something sour, what could I have done? You can't just leave your father to die in the desert after twenty-six years without him. Surely Duncan would have understood that.

I made my father a set of keys for the house. Silver for the front door, gold for the back. He could never remember which key was which, and so most days he would press the doorbell in a perky three-ring succession.

"I made you keys," I would say as I opened the door.

"I know. But I just can't remember which one is which," he'd say, giving me an impish smile. Sometimes he'd leave the keys at home in the morning. I'd find them under a stack of newspapers or wadded up in an old lunch sack beneath the kitchen table.

"Sometime I might not be home when you lock yourself out," I chastised.

"Ohhhh, you're always home," he said, his hair greased in rigid lines over his thinning pate.

He was a very messy man, my father. He'd leave the

olive oil on the counter, bags of herbs strewn around it like windblown trash. His socks gathered in heaps and his bedroom began to smell sweet and fetid. While I brushed my teeth that strong, footy smell would waft through the door. When he went to work, I gathered up armfuls of his dirty laundry and threw it in the washer. I stripped his filthy sheets, dotted with toenails and hair, gathered the damp towels, straightened the stacks of papers and magazines. When he came home, he'd either pretend not to notice, or he really didn't notice, that the room was orderly and aired out. This, more than the fact that I cleaned his bedroom in the first place, always infuriated me, causing me to bang pans around while cooking and burn my hand on the oven rack.

And then my father began to bring home friends—large, pomaded men from the garage suffering from various degrees of bowleggedness.

"Hey, it's the missus!" they'd cry when they stomped in, dragging their oily fingers against the white walls. They'd gather on my small back patio, smoke cigarettes, and drink beer until the moon hung bright above them. I tried not to listen to them talk, but words slipped through the screen, over the tiles and into the kitchen. Women, car payments, garage politics.

I purchased a pair of earplugs. Fancy ones made out of an expanding gelatin. I worked in my kitchen and pretended they weren't there. But eventually more and more friends began to appear. My father was popular, I realized. Ten friends crammed on the back patio gave way to fifteen. Then twenty. Brothers and cousins of the bowlegged men spilled down the patio steps, into the small parking lot I shared with my neighbor.

"Look," I told him one night when he came in to go to the bathroom. "We have to discuss this." I gestured toward the mob of greasy heads bobbing outside the kitchen window. My father paused, furrowed his brows.

"This isn't your personal ballroom," I told him. "You can't just invite the entire garage over every night."

"It's not every night," he said, wiping his brow with his forearm. "I have to go to the bathroom."

He began to walk away.

"No! Wait a minute. It's *my* bathroom, *my* house. You're *staying* here. You can't just do whatever you want whenever you want. There need to be rules," I said.

He blinked incredulously at me.

"Rules?" he asked.

"Rules," I said.

"What kind of rules?" His blue eyes turned one shade darker.

"Rules," I said, "so that I can get something done around here. Not everyone in the world has your hours."

"I'm your father," he said gravely. "Watch how you talk to me."

"You may be my father," I said, "but you're making me crazy."

"Ah, well, family's like a tin of nuts—"

"No, really," I said. "Really, you can't just come in here and take over everything. I spend hours every morning bleaching oil stains off the walls. If this doesn't stop, you're going to have to find somewhere else to live."

He looked at me, then at the floor. He raised his dirt-lined hand to his hair and stood with one palm pressed against the back of his head.

"Are you threatening me?" he finally asked.

Again I thought of Duncan. Some people go chasing these phantoms all of their lives. Each day begins with a shadow of loss that hangs with the curtains, each evening comes to a close with a list of ways things could have been. And here was my answer to all of that, standing puzzled and wounded in front of me.

"Maybe I am," I said to him.

He entered the bathroom. I sat reading the same line over and over again. The men outside laughed big full laughs and a bottle of liquor broke on the cement.

When my father came out of the bathroom, his cheeks hung sadly. "I'll tell them all to leave," he said, and walked slowly out the door.

Soon the men went back to wherever they came from and my father traipsed in, closing the door with a pathetic click. He gave me a hurt look as he wandered past me into the living room.

The next few days my father returned from work silently, sighing and shifting in boredom. He would examine the contents of the fridge, pick up each container individually, and then set it back down. He'd get out a deck of cards, sit next to me, and shuffle them. He brought home a book of word finds.

"Can't anyone else have people over?" I finally asked. "Why don't some of your friends ever have parties?"

He shrugged. "Doesn't work like that."

The morose mood that settled over him made him even more of a slob. Dirty Q-tips appeared behind the bathroom trash can. Beer cans wedged between the sofa cushions. Each morning I wandered the house with a mug of coffee, picking up the residue of his depression, burning piñon incense and scented candles. The house reeked of feet, earth, and flowers. The dog began to sleep with one paw draped over his snout. I began to get head-aches.

And then the phone calls started. Hour after hour, the phone rang, even when my father was at work.

"Is your father around?" the voices would ask. Men, women, even small children called. I took messages for him in a spiral notebook. I filled one, then another. At night he sat in his bedroom, the phone dragged in, and returned phone calls. Who did he talk to all those nights, hunched over in his pungent bedroom? I didn't ask, and he didn't tell me.

The mood was tense and the air thick. The dog began to tremble in his sleep. His tags rattled. I stroked his ears but couldn't soothe him, and soon he trembled all the time. It interfered with his eating. Then one day I let him out in the yard for a minute, and when I went out to fetch him, he was gone.

Sometimes you lose something—an earring, a sweater—and you have a sharp hope that it will turn up. I walked every street of the neighborhood hollering for him. I hung bright yellow posters of his face on lampposts, on bulletin boards at the grocery, lunch counter, and nearby church. I even prayed. But the loss felt final. Infinite.

"Look what you've done!" I said to my father, my voice breaking.

"I wasn't even home when it happened. I didn't *do* any-thing," he said.

"He couldn't deal with the tension."

"What are you talking about?"

"All the phone calls, the crap everywhere—"

"I think you have a stress problem," he said, turning

toward the fridge to grab a beer. "You need to chill out or you'll die young."

"Wouldn't that be a blessing," I said, slamming out to the yard to fume and miss my dog.

I went to the pound every other day, just in case he'd been brought there without his tags. I became friendly with the woman behind the counter.

"Sorry, hon," she'd say when I opened the door, the bells on the handle dinging. "No beagles today." I walked the strip of cages, looking at all the dogs, their dark, shining eyes pleading or distrustful. The plaintive barks reverberated off my body.

I was looking at my favorite dog—a runt with a bad case of mange but a sweet, polite bark, when I felt this cool, highly charged wind pass behind me. It felt like a ghost, or what I imagined a ghost felt like, passing by in a tunnel of barking dogs. I turned to see.

He looked older, his hair short and his arms long. His shoulders stooped; I didn't remember this about him.

"Duncan?" I said, walking toward him. He looked over. He seemed not to recognize me. But quickly, his face broke into a grin.

"No way," he said. "No way." His crooked teeth made him look honest. We went out for coffee.

Duncan was always a beautiful boy, and he grew into a beautiful man. His skin shone like copper rocks in a river and his eyes had this feline watchfulness, green as those bright spots in the sea. He had moved with Lucy to Santa Fe. She wanted to open a jewelry store, but the money got tight and the relationship fizzled and he moved back to Arizona.

"I wanted to call you," he said sheepishly, "but I was too

ashamed." My heart soared and plunged; I felt a little sick. Duncan was peering at me from over his coffee cup. I tried not to look at him, taking stock of the cars in the lot. Three red ones in a row, flanked by trucks. A nice, cosmic symmetry. And then, suddenly, he laughed.

"I'm sorry," he said. "Tell me about yourself, what you've been up to."

I looked at him.

"Well," I said, "for starters, I found my father." Duncan's hands tightened around his coffee mug; I watched to see if he would move them, but they remained still.

"What do you mean?" he asked gravely.

"Just that," I said. "I mean I found him."

"I thought he was dead."

"So did I."

Several women in bright windbreakers came through the door, noisily making their way to the end of the counter.

"So he wasn't dead?" Duncan asked skeptically.

"Duncan, I really don't know."

A debate brewed inside him. Did he not believe me?

"Okay," he said decisively. "You found him. That's great! You know, you look good," he said, leaning back in his chair. "You look really happy. Your skin and your hair. That must be it, right? Your father."

I tried to tell him the story, but he seemed pained and I felt like I needed to edit every detail.

"I'd love to meet him," Duncan said, leaning across the table to take my hand. "I mean, if that would be okay with you."

He was testing me. In Duncan's world, fathers died and stayed dead. They left regrets in boxes of journals, mean mementos to remind the living of the futility of life.

"Well, he works a lot," I said. Duncan nodded slowly. "But I suppose we could work something out. If you really wanted to. I mean, if you think—"

"I want to," Duncan said. "I want to, really."

We traded phone numbers and I returned to my house, a crazy shaking in my arms that wouldn't stop.

My deadlines loomed, but I couldn't settle down to work. I turned on the television in the living room. I turned on the radio in the kitchen. I turned on all the lights. I started the dishwasher. I cleaned out the fridge.

I was repotting every plant in the house when my father walked in. A strange thing happened then. I looked at his face, really looked at it. His skin puffed around his eyes. His stubble was dark and thick. Lines deepened further into his brow, touchable, traceable lines that grew shallow and almost imperceptible before his receding hairline began. His eyes were a brilliant, pale blue, too shocking for his plain face. And his lips—his lips were so pink. It hurt my heart to look at them.

My father, I thought, incredulously. My father.

I crouched over my African violet, soil wedged beneath my fingernails. There was suddenly so much I wanted to say to him. About living without him all of my life, about finding him, about the obvious stress this put on our relationship, about his life before me, about my life before him—

My father went to the fridge and took out a beer. He set the cap on top of the fridge, tipped his head back, and took a long, deep swig. Slowly, looking straight into my eyes, he swallowed and let out a rolling burp. Without saying anything, he kicked off his shoes and plodded into the living room.

The feeling of tenderness vanished.

I squeezed my hands into fists and then flattened them against my thighs. I still felt jumpy and wanted to tell someone about finding Duncan.

I walked into the living room and stood behind the chair where my father sat, his ankles crossed, watching baseball bloopers. He pretended not to notice me.

Waves of nervousness started in my stomach. I went back into the kitchen to make some peppermint tea.

The trash can was full to bursting. The beer, which took up an entire shelf of the fridge, had forced the bread onto the counter, the bottles of juice into the laundry room. I had taken to buying potato chips and mayonnaise, things I had ruled out long ago. I set up a workstation beneath the kitchen window, since my father had taken over my office. So much had shifted in such a short time. I began to drum my fingers on the table. My father began foraging for dinner. Leftover Chinese food, cheese, applesauce.

I didn't know where to begin.

"Dad," I imagined saying. But I hadn't been calling him that. "Father," I would say. "Father, I have this friend I would like you to meet." How contrived. I couldn't say that. We didn't have that kind of thing going. I'd just have to bring Duncan over and hope for the best.

My father was busy making some sort of Chinese food melt in the toaster oven. The smell reminded me of my missing dog.

"How was your day?" I asked.

"Who wants to know?" he asked.

"I do," I said.

"Fine," he said.

"Great," I said.

"Gross, there's rice in the silverware drawer," he said. "Yuck."

"I have an idea. You could clean it!"

My father began to scratch his inner thigh. I drummed my fingers again. The phone rang. My father turned, his face lit up, and he trotted off.

There's no way in, I thought hopelessly. My father. How embarrassing. What would I tell Duncan? "I'm ashamed of him, Duncan. All of your life, you've wanted a father and now I have mine and I don't want anyone to see him."

He stalked back into the kitchen.

"Phone's for you." The receiver smelled faintly of beer breath.

"Hello?" I asked.

"Was that him?" Duncan whispered.

"Yeah," I said.

"That's amazing," he said. I pressed my fingernail into the plastic crease that held the two halves of the phone receiver together. "Sorry to break the three-day etiquette thing, but I figured I knew you well enough to call when I wanted to."

"Oh. Sure," I said.

"So, I was thinking about having breakfast at the lunch counter near your house on Saturday, I guess that's tomorrow, and I was thinking that would be a great time for us all to get together."

I looked over at my father, who was standing, hypnotized, in front of the television. He turned off all the lights; the colors from the screen bathed him in reds and blues. It made him look spooky.

"Tomorrow?" I asked.

"Yeah, how does that sound?"

"Duncan, I don't know how to say this but—"

"What?" Duncan asked.

"Well. It's just that things have been topsy-turvy."

"Don't overthink it," he said. "You guys just meet me at the counter at eleven. That's not too late, right?"

Now I was in a bind. I could show up alone and Duncan would think I had been lying; I could stand him up and it would seem like I had been lying; or I could bring my father and hope that he behaved, well, fatherly.

"Hey," I said to my father after Duncan hung up. "We have breakfast plans." He glanced over his shoulder at me.

"Says who?"

"Says Duncan." My father looked at me blankly. "My ex-boyfriend."

"You had a boyfriend?" my father sneered.

"We're meeting at the lunch counter at eleven tomorrow."

"Fine with me," he said, cracking his knuckles.

I looked at the lines of my father's body. Though not a tall man, he did have a sort of presence. His build didn't indicate a delicate spine—no gorgeously stacked vertebrae. Instead he looked bolstered up by a large pole of metal.

I thought about the way that blood goes through the body. The liquid seems to know exactly which way to go, as if every cell in the body has a tiny, thoughtful brain. I thought of my father's blood, my father's bones, the ligaments that held him upright like that, his arms crossed, his legs apart.

How smart the body is. I closed my eyes and felt my

own blood racing through my veins, making my hands and feet warm. I wished I could ask those tiny brains what to do.

My father's Chinese food melt lay half eaten on a plate on the coffee table. Some noodles had fallen to the floor, glued there by orange cheese. He'd already gone through two beers, the bottles wedged haphazardly between the couch and the wall. His socks, as usual, had been tossed like bait into the center of the room.

In that moment, my impatience with him ebbed. I wasn't filled with a strong, peaceful love or anything. I just felt resigned. And this felt like progress.

"So, eleven, then," I said. "I guess we'll just walk over there a little before, okay?"

My father didn't turn around. "Whatever you say. You're the boss around here." He changed the channel. Strange shadows came and went.

"I guess I'm going to bed now," I said. "Good night."

"Mhmm," went my father and then guffawed at the commercial.

I felt heavy and empty; I lay in bed for a long time without sleeping. I would get up in the morning, clean the house, get dressed, have coffee so I was alert for the lunch counter encounter. Somewhere, in between thoughts, I fell asleep.

I woke exhausted, a feeling of failure in my bones. I looked at the clock. Ten-thirty.

"Shit," I said, throwing myself out of bed. "Fuck fuck fuck." I threw on a robe and dashed into the bathroom. I began to strip off my pajamas when I realized that the bathroom was spotless—the sink wiped clean, the toilet seat down. The razor and shaving cream that usually crowded my toothbrush jar off the shelf were gone. I put my robe back on and went to find my father.

Each room was completely clean. I knocked on my father's door.

"Father?" I called. And then, "Dad?"

I cracked it open. My father's Tupperware storage containers of clothes and shoes were gone. The notebooks of his phone messages, also gone. Only the futon remained, sheetless, and the empty bookshelf.

I went back into the living room and sat on the couch. I thought of Duncan waiting expectantly for me at the lunch counter and me without a father to prove myself by.

"He's gone," I'd say. "I woke up this morning and he vanished as suddenly as he came, like a dream father." Duncan would look sorry for me, but not in the right way. "But," I'd say, "it wasn't a dream."

The stillness of the house clung to my skin, sticky and disconcerting.

I worked myself into a panic, searching the house for details that would prove that I had had a father. He couldn't just come into my life, turn my house on its head, and then vanish without a trace. There had to be a note, a photograph, something.

My head began to pound. I was frantically turning the sofa cushions over, looking for beer bottles and petrified cheese when I heard it, a soft whimpering coming from the side door. For a moment I couldn't move. And then I walked over and placed my cheek against the cool whiteness of the door.

WHERE NOTHING IS

I T'S THE WATCHES AGAIN. DRAPED ON THE EDGE OF THE
bathtub like that, they look like little corpses. And in the
bedroom, it's the ties. Two dozen lie across the soft lace
bedspread: yellow paisley, turquoise polka dot, ducks flying on a flat navy sky. Neil's father, Geoff, was a loud
dresser. And a pack rat.

"How long is this going to last?" I ask our dog, Winston, as I roll each tie into a coil. Winston flops down on
the rug and sighs.

Two years before Geoff, Neil's father, died, Mindy,
Neil's mother, caught him in bed with one of his students.
Geoff taught sociology at the junior college. The young
woman was twenty. Mindy said, "All I saw were her
legs."

Sometimes I try to re-create the scene, using just that
detail. Mindy stopped home to get the sneakers she forgot;
she was on her way to the gym between appointments. She
wore spandex leggings and a fuzzy blue headband. Geoff
must have been on top (which makes sense given the age

thing, the power inequity), overwhelming the girl, whose legs were curled around his thick middle.

It can't be true that she saw *only* the girl's legs. She must have seen her feet, too. And Geoff's legs. And probably his rear. Or maybe they were under the covers, the girl's legs sticking out, and they really were all she saw.

Mindy apparently said "Pardon me" and left the house, returning the next day to pack clothes and dishes in a dozen huge boxes. She never returned.

Neil hasn't forgiven her for not coming to Geoff's deathbed. But Mindy was steadfast.

"He made his decision," she kept saying. So Neil went to the hospital every day without her.

When Neil has bad days, he sits on the sofa playing with the cord of the blinds. He stares at the princess tree in front of our apartment, stares into the wood like he is going to infiltrate it. He locks his large jaw and looks petulant— thirteen instead of thirty.

Then the objects start to appear. His father's junk—the ties, the watches, the collection of leftist pamphlets from the 1950s. There's a box of argyle vests, a box of tweed jackets, a box of ski hats. When I get home from work the kitchen looks like a tag sale, objects arranged with like objects, sometimes in subcategories of color, sometimes just flung out of the boxes at random.

Five months ago, a month before Geoff's death, I met Gwen Eliot, a friend of a friend who'd recently moved to the Bay Area. I didn't think much of her, but Neil liked her immediately. I'd come home from work to find Gwen and Neil in the midst of a poker game or making deviled eggs.

Now she calls nearly every weekend to go for walks with Winston or to ride pedal boats out at the pond. Lately, plans with Gwen have gotten more involved. Last weekend she and Neil took a surfing lesson (Gwen claimed her voucher was good for only two people, not three) while I sat on the windy beach in my sweater, trying to keep my magazine's pages flat.

That's where he is tonight. "At movies with G," his note reads. "Midnight showing." I wad up the note and leave it on the vanity. It's the third note this week.

When I wake up in the morning, the box of ties is gone and Winston slaps his tail happily against my head. Neil's next to me in bed, the newspaper unfolded in front of him, though he's staring at me. The sun hits his eyelashes and they look bleached, almost yellow. His Adam's apple jiggles slightly.

"What's going on?" I ask. Winston, pleased that I am finally awake, stands and rubs his cold nose in my eye.

"It's a gorgeous day," Neil says. Light soaks our sheer curtains; the white walls bang with it.

"It's California," I say. "It's always a gorgeous day." But that doesn't dampen his desire to go out, and before I can put in my two cents, he's on the phone with Gwen.

"I want to get out of the city," Gwen says. She hasn't touched her sandwich. It sits there, pale as her skin. "You wouldn't believe the freaks I had to deal with this morning. One woman started screaming that she saw me put nut powder in her garden shake. *I'm allergic to nuts!* God.

And then I said someone put nut powder in something she ate long before I did and I got a lecture from Rushelle on customer service."

Neil snorts.

"Let's get the hell out of Dodge."

"Where do you want to go?" I ask.

"Someplace scary," Gwen says.

Winston waits patiently under a tree in the parking lot. Neil unties him and they climb into the backseat together. The dark vinyl is so hot that it takes a minute to settle on the seats. A rich doggy smell abounds. We roll down the windows.

Gwen turns on the radio. She's an aspiring actress. Her next audition, she announced over lunch, is for a Christian channel planning a new drama about "the angels that live within." (Who knows how her agent swung that one— Gwen's got dark wiry hair and a soaring Jewish nose.) She trains by listening to the evangelical stations. Today a deep, resonant voice is saying: *You must know. You must know in your heart how to walk alongside him. With faith, the Scripture tells us. Walk with faith. You may question that word, but it is not to be questioned. See the light in faith!*

We take 80 out of Berkeley and follow it east. We drive and drive. Gwen wants to find a place where nothing is.

"Light in faith," she booms.

I turn off the radio. She shrugs and puts her feet on the dashboard, grabs her front tooth with her fingers. Neil and Gwen begin a rousing round of Mustache, No Mustache. A BMW convertible pulls up beside us and they both scream "No mustache!" But they're wrong. The man has a full beard that seems to begin right under his eyes.

"Damn," Neil says.

"Maybe we should just pull off on one of these farm roads," Neil says after a while.

"Yeah," Gwen says, letting go of her tooth.

I pull off. We drive out past some fields, fenced with barbed wire. After a while, the fences give way and we drive down a dirt road through corn, then through something I don't recognize.

"Turn down there," Gwen says. After a mile or two, we pull over. Shrubby plants grow on either side of us. It's not scary here. Everything is in rows. Gwen gets out of the car.

"Is this soy?" she bellows, her thin mouth thinning further with the effort, her eyes bugging. Then she starts to cackle. She learned this exercise in acting school. Scream what should be quiet.

Neil unzips his pants and pees on the crop.

"Gross," says Gwen. "Some family is going to eat that."

"Or some cow," Neil says.

"It's better than the shit they're spraying on it," I say.

"What're we going to do?" Neil asks. He looks boyish in his wrinkled hiking pants and pea green shirt. He looks fun.

Sometimes I catch Neil looking at Gwen and I see a fog there, like he's imagining what it would be like to cross the invisible border that separates one person from another. Neil and I have been together so long that when he looks at Gwen like that, I find I'm curious, as if part of my own body has sloughed off and is misbehaving.

Even so, when Gwen takes off her shirt, I feel a kick of dread.

"Let's run naked through the soy!" she says. Gwen has a scar on her stomach from a surgery she had during adolescence. It's shiny and pink, like burnished stoneware. Her bra's a complicated crimson number with cheap lace and a little black bow between her breasts. When she takes off her shorts, her underwear matches. Maybe she planned this naked outing just to show off her fashion sense.

Neil looks like he's about to sink into the gravel. His hands go to block his crotch. "I'm going for a walk," he says.

"I'm not getting undressed," I say to Gwen.

"Suit yourself," she says, sliding out of her underwear. Her dark pubic hair is shaved into a stripe. And then she takes off her bra, revealing the large silver hoop in her nipple. Leave it to Gwen not to stop at a tiny ring. She does a little bunny hop and the ring swings up and down as she lands. She slides her painted toenails back into her ballet flats and prances through the shrubby plants, waving her arms around. Winston barks big, hollow barks from the backseat of the car.

"Let Winston out!" Gwen calls. I do and he runs after Gwen, trying to figure out what to make of it all.

It's possible, people say, that the only available meaning is in the moment: the field, the sun on my dark hair, the wiggle of Gwen's fleshy ass. Existence is its own reward. No one on earth is having a moment quite like mine. This is my prize: a boyfriend obsessed with his dead dad's watches, hiding his erection behind the car, and a friend whom I really can't stand.

Winston has regained an ounce of puppyhood. He crouches and jumps against naked Gwen as she leaps around. A few pink welts appear on her stomach where his claws scrape. She laughs and growls at the dog.

"That's not a great idea, Gwen," I say. She smiles, dimples sucking into her face.

"A-rrrrrrrr," she says to Winston.

"Grrr-arrrr," Winston says back to her. Gwen gets on her knees and pushes Winston's head down with her hands. The dog pops up and barks joyfully, then picks up a long, misshapen pod and shakes it in his jaws. Gwen grabs it and holds it above Winston's head. I imagine Winston putting his furry arms around Gwen, leaning in toward her, their tongues entwined, the two of them toppling over in bestial bliss. How jealous would Neil be? And then it's all pretty fast—a scream and blood on Gwen's hand and the dog running off to cower near the car.

"OhmyGod," she says.

Neil comes out from the crop. "What's happening?"

Gwen is making little gasping noises. Her bottom lip keeps drooping, exposing her lower teeth. She takes her hand off her breast and there's blood all over it. The silver hoop glitters beneath her on the dirt.

"Fucking dog," she cries.

Neil goes over to the car, takes Winston's towel out, and delivers it to Gwen, who bunches it up and sticks it on her ripped nipple.

"Ow," she gasps.

I can't move. If I move, I'm afraid I'll do what I'm tempted to do, which is laugh.

"Just sit for a minute," Neil says. But already I hear a motor coming from somewhere.

"Fuck," Gwen says, stumbling up. There's dirt on her pale legs. A little strand of foliage hangs from her pubic stripe. She hunches over herself. Neil grabs her pants and shirt, and as he hands them to her, we see the tractor turning down the road.

Winston lies down. He rests his head on his paws and makes guilty, sorry eyes.

"Can you do something?" Neil says to me.

"What do you want me to do?" I ask.

"Well, help her."

"Hold this for me," Gwen says, gesturing to the towel wadded on her breast. I hold the towel in place as she steps into her jeans and will myself to behave.

"What the hell is going on here," the man on the tractor yells. He cuts the engine and swings himself down from the high seat. "My guys said they saw some car turn down here. This is private property." He's bright red—from his hair to his face to his T-shirt—and he's sweating. He tromps down the road.

"Fuck," Gwen whispers and bats my hand away.

"What in God's name?" the man says.

I silently dare Gwen to do it, to drop the towel and scream *"Is this your soy, sir?"* But I know she's got that joie de vivre only when it comes to Neil. Her one bare breast stands out, brave survivor that it is. The man stares.

"We were lost," Gwen says. The man nods and looks over at Neil.

"Get out of here," he says.

"I'm sorry." Neil opens the back door of the car. "Winston," he calls.

The man walks into the crop a little way to see if we've damaged anything—or to see if we've planted little devils there.

"I got your license plate. If I find anything wrong, I have a brother at the sheriff's."

We drive silently back toward Berkeley. Every few miles Neil leans forward to ask Gwen how she's doing.

*   *   *

The first affair my father had was with my baby-sitter when I was ten. My mom was training to be a nurse and worked nights. Cassie, a student at the local university, had thick caramel-colored bangs and a swimmer's body. At first, Cassie would leave when my dad arrived. Then she started staying for dinner. Usually, when my dad came home, he ignored me, poured some bourbon, and sat by the stereo listening to Motown. So it thrilled me to stay up playing Monopoly with them, night after night. My dad groaned theatrically when I bought a hotel on Park Place. "She's a real entrepreneur!" he said. "A real go-getter!" He tousled my hair, just like dads in commercials. Cassie giggled, tilted her head back, opening her mouth slightly. During those long Monopoly games, she always laughed with her tongue slightly out.

I don't remember what I knew about sex at the time. But I remember being sent to my room. I was playing veterinarian and in a well-meaning frenzy I cut off a stuffed beaver's ear with my mom's pinking shears. I wandered into the hall, panicked, beaver in hand. My father and Cassie were in the office with the door closed. I could hear Cassie sighing.

"That's it," my dad was saying. "That's it, that's it."

Did this change the course of my life? At ten, was my fate sealed? I know something will happen between Gwen and Neil. It feels like I've known this since the day we first kissed. His lips met mine and my body went toward his and somewhere a tiny sign lit up. "Gwen!" the sign said, though this was years before we'd met her. Jasmine! Katie! Paula!

My mother caught my dad. I don't know how. But they

fought and saw a counselor, and for a little while I had to see one, too. She wore loose purple dresses and we sat on the floor on cushions. Then he had an affair with my mom's friend Sally. That led to some EST thing. Then we had money trouble. Then he disappeared with the EST woman for almost six months when I was in high school.

Sometimes I want to tell Neil just to get it over with. Or I want to change the rules of the game to make it permissible. This has been my mother's tactic. Her hair is long and peppered with gray. Before this, when it fell long and auburn down her back, I imagine that she used to lean in toward my dad, laugh when he told jokes. Now she is wry. She pulls one side of her lips into a smile, but her eyes never match it.

People bustle through the crowded emergency room and, given the nature of Gwen's injury, we're low on the list of priorities. We settle into blue upholstered chairs. She's in a better mood now. The breast hurts, she says, but it's stopped searing.

"Man, did you see the face on that farmer?" Neil laughs.

"God, it was almost worth it, just for that," Gwen says.

"Get *out* of here," Neil mimics loudly. Gwen beams at him. I lean away from a man who's muttering in the seat next to me, and as I do, Neil grabs my hand. "Jesus," he says, and absently kisses the top of my head. Gwen looks away, toward the wall of pastel prints.

"Actually it still really hurts," she says, standing. "Maybe these assholes can get me some painkillers."

At the front desk, we see Gwen lift her T-shirt. The receptionist shakes her head, but a nurse off to the side says something and Gwen disappears behind some swinging doors.

"I'm starving," Neil says.

"Do you think she'll get stitches?"

Neil winces. "I really don't want to think about it."

We buy Cheetos and a granola bar from the vending machine. Forty-five minutes later, Gwen comes out looking exhausted.

"Hi, Neeeeel," she says. Her body is lax; she practically staggers toward him.

"What'd they give you, Gwen?" he asks. She winks at him and then gives me an appraising look.

"I'm pretty out of it," she says. She steps next to Neil and grabs his arm. "Steady," she says to no one in particular.

She's sure to show us the breast before she goes upstairs to her apartment. We walk her to the ornate arch over her building and her eyelids sink down her medicated eyes. She lifts her blouse and there it is, covered in layers of gauze. I hope it hurts like hell in the morning. I hope the whole thing falls off. Of course, Gwen leaves the shirt up long enough that we can both take in the other breast, which is perfect and whole, a guiding light to the injured.

Gwen must imagine the following scene:

I start for the car, and when my back is turned Neil puts a gentle palm around Gwen's uninjured breast. He lifts it slightly and bends, his full lips searching it out. He says, "Wait here."

"I'm going to help Gwen into bed," he says as he opens the car door for me. Earnestness blares from his bright eyes. "Take the car. I'll get a cab."

I nod. I can't stop it. The damage has already been done.

Upstairs, Gwen lights a candle by her bed. Her body is warm, full of candles, full of light. The pain feels distant and a version of it travels down, ending in an ache between her legs. She looks at Neil, peels off her shirt, her pants. Again she's naked in front of him.

This time there's no need to hide behind a plant. Neil lets Gwen take off his clothes. He runs his hands down her good breast, careful not to touch the other. Then with this in mind, he turns her around, lowers her onto all fours, lifts her butt into the air. He cups the one good breast as he situates himself inside her.

I don't feel like talking on the way home. Neil taps a song on the steering wheel with his thumbs. He cracks the window and his curls blow toward me.

Neil hasn't forgiven his mother. Mindy leaves messages on our voice mail during the day, when she knows he'll be at work. *Call when you want to,* she says. *I love you.* He claims he's through with her.

I ran into her a few months ago at the grocery. She wore a sheer red top beneath her blazer. Her face shone with makeup. She stopped her cart near a wall of bread and gave me a long hug.

"How's Neil?" she asked.

"He's coping," I said. Mindy's cart held a whole roasted chicken, a bottle of wine, some flowers. As I stood chatting with her, a man with owl-framed glasses approached. His gray hair stuck out from his head like he'd just been licked by a giant tongue.

"Darling," he said to Mindy, "I couldn't find that coffee."

＊   ＊   ＊

That night, Winston jumps into bed. He looks deeply at Neil and Neil looks back. I take the newspaper and set it between us. Neil pets Winston's ears.

"Sometimes I see my dad looking back at me," Neil says. I look at Winston's dark eyes and for a moment, I can see Geoff, too. His silent pleading toward the end, when he could no longer talk, when he might have said anything. Finally Winston can't stand it anymore and he hops off the bed to lie on the floor.

If I focus, I can hear the watches ticking from where Neil has put them on the dresser. Neil never fixes the time on them, though he winds them before he sets them in their rows. Geoff must have glanced at those watches thousands of times. I wonder if he ever imagined their life after him.

"I would never do that to you," Neil says. "I know there's part of you that thinks I would." For a moment, I find this switch confusing. He scoots toward me, smashing newspaper beneath him. I try to pry the newspaper out but it's stuck. Winston whines. He's noticed an old bone under the dresser and looks to me for help or approval.

"Do you believe me?" Neil asks.

He crawls on top of me. I hold his ears, put my forehead against his, and feel the bone there.

THE EGG GAME

URI KEEPS THE EGG NEAR HIS KEYBOARD AS HE returns phone calls. Half of it sticks out of the hole India cut in the pink sock. "You think we're going to lay down and die? Just like that?" the attorney screeches, his voice tinny through the receiver. Uri runs a forefinger around the spot where shell meets polyester. As the lawyer starts in on the points of his counteroffer (five hundred dollars instead of twenty-two thousand), Uri takes a red felt-tip pen and draws a little face on it. Two round eyes with long lashes and a mouth shaped like a heart. It doesn't look like a baby; it looks lascivious. He takes the egg out of the sock and flips it to its clean side. This time, with a black Sharpie, he makes round eyes with little dots in them, a small horseshoe-shaped nose, and a smile. It's no infant, but it's an improvement.

Blithe comes in as he's hanging up. She's wearing a red silk shirt with a plunging neckline. A little pearl buries itself in her cleavage.

"Did I do this right?" she asks, placing a memorandum on his desk. She always wears her hair in a giant cascade. Locks of orange curls tumble over her cheeks and shoulders while the rest of her hair sits heaped on top in an arrangement of glittery hair clips. He can smell her shampoo—something with fruit in it—pear.

"It looks good," Uri says. (Why wouldn't it? He e-mailed his template to her and she hasn't changed anything.) He notices a run in her panty hose; it starts inside her little black heel, creeps up her inner calf and thigh, and disappears beneath her pleated skirt.

Blithe hasn't figured out that this is a dead-end job. She's twenty-five and uses her government paychecks to buy manicures, lip gloss, and a wide variety of silk shirts. She keeps her plastic federal investigator badge on her desk, propped up like a holiday greeting, and bought the fanciest gold-embossed business cards—the ones with the federal seal that cost extra. All the guys in the office want to do her, but no one says it. They can't say it. They work at the Equal Employment Opportunity Commission. That would be in direct conflict with Title VII of the Civil Rights Act of 1964. You cannot discriminate on the basis of sex. If you want to fuck Blithe, you better want to fuck everyone, regardless of gender. You better want to fuck your stubborn wife in those baggy pants she refuses to take off and that terrible shapeless pink sweater.

"You want a mint?" Blithe asks, holding out a small tin. Then she sees it. "What is that?" she asks. "An egg?"

"Don't ask."

Blithe sucks on her mint and casts a dubious glance at the egg.

Uri hates fluorescent lighting, preferring to work under a lamp in the shape of a goose, a present from his wife. Sometimes when Blithe comes in she leans over to touch it as if it might be alive.

Now she asks, "Did the goose lay it?" Uri closes the document on his computer. "Nice smiley face, anyway," she says. "Is it for lunch?"

"I didn't bring lunch," Uri says, rolling his chair back. This segues into a conversation about good lunch spots in the area, then into a plan. They eat at the pasta shop a block away. Blithe orders a salad and eats demurely. When he casts his eyes toward his pasta, he can glimpse a tiny bit of black lace through a gap in her shirt buttons. He allows himself to imagine her breasts, freed from their lacy harness. Her nipples would probably be light in color, girlish. She'd be sweating, but only slightly, only enough to make her gleam. Then a tomato slides off Blithe's fork and lands on her skirt.

"Oh damn," she says, picking it up with her fingernails. "I'm such a slob."

Blithe's originally from Atlanta. She's got a faint southern lilt that's immediately endearing. She tells him about her new apartment—a studio, small but just redone. She mentions the man she went out with a few times who turned out to be gay. "He was *just double checking*. That's what he said, I swear." Recently she'd broken things off with another man she met at a party who seemed perfect, an attorney at a big firm downtown. He had a cabin up at Tahoe and a purebred weimaraner that brought him his newspaper in the morning. "His wife left him for a transsexual—that's the right term for someone who's in the process of changing, right? Before I moved here I didn't know anything about this stuff. Anyway. He had anger issues. One time his dog peed in the hall and he lost it—hit it over and over and over again with the newspaper until the dog was just quivering." She presses a glass of water against her cheek and it leaves a small wet spot. "This city's a joke for regular girls." Blithe sets her fork down and clasps her hands in her lap. She pushes her feet against the floor so the chair tips back. "You must get tired of all the ladies chasing you around," she says. She lets the chair slam back to the ground and leans forward so that her face is close to his. Her eyes flash.

India is meditating when he comes home. The dark living room feels overly warm. She's on a folded blanket, her dark hair frizzing in a triangular shape around her head. Slowly she turns, stretches. They have a pact that he won't talk to her for ten minutes after "her quiet." Usually he doesn't mind, but today it irritates him.

"How's it going?" he chirps. He sets the egg down on the coffee table. India shoots him a disapproving look. He shrugs off his raincoat and goes to the bedroom to lie down.

"What's the matter?" she asks. At least she's out of those pants. She's wearing the stretchy yoga pants he likes, tight around her thighs and butt.

"Nothing," he says. He doesn't mean it to sound peevish—in fact, he's just about to hold out his hands to her when she rolls her eyes and leaves.

Uri knows how they got here. He's not dim like his brother, who never seems to know why he's fighting with his wife. Uri and India are fighting, and have been for weeks, because Uri said that he was tired of her excuses, that she was thirty-five years old and he was thirty-seven and if they wanted to have a baby—to have the two babies they'd agreed to when they got married—they needed to hop to it. India said he had to be patient. She wanted to finish her book. When he asked how long that would take, her nostrils flared, her voice soared to a very high pitch, and she accused him of lacking a critical kind of faith in her. Then Uri read part of the novel.

"You read it?" she gasped when he told her. "It's a draft! It's not ready for anyone to see!"

The truth was, though he was nicer than this to her face, the novel was terrible. It was about two sisters after they lose their father. India's father died a year before she started writing and versions of her childhood memories came whizzing from the mouths of ten-year-olds.

The fight has since changed direction. India now claims that Uri isn't responsible (for example, he left the barbecue out half the winter and now the little piece around the starter is rusted) and that the baby will require more selflessness than he anticipates.

"You couldn't just leave a baby on the coffee table," she says to him when she comes back in the bedroom.

"Really?" he says.

"In fact," she says, "you couldn't just take a baby to work like that. It would cry."

"It's not a baby, India. It's an egg." She shoots him a withering look.

"Maybe we should attach an alarm clock to it," she says. "It could go off like every twenty minutes and you'd have to feed it through a tube coming out of your shirt."

"What's this about?" Uri says, sitting up. "Do you not want to have kids?"

"I want to have kids," she says. "But I want to be sure you're ready to be selfless. I don't want to give over my entire life like Melody and Kim. I don't want to stay at home watching my husband go out for beers with friends while I wipe green poo off my fingers and rub cream on my chapped nipples. I like my nipples. I *like* my life. And I want to finish my book."

When he first met India, she wore her dark curls trapped in thick braids, bound with silly plastic doodads. She drank vodka and cherry Coke at three in the afternoon. To celebrate their second anniversary, she made him a scavenger hunt. She painted small clues on little circles of paper, hid them around the neighborhood, and at the end seduced him in a grass field behind the supermarket. He thinks of her drinking her weekend coffee with vanilla ice cream floating in it, chattering about the movie reviews, the cold weather outside, her split ends. Despite her charms, it's hard not to strangle her.

For dinner India makes a frittata. He notices that she's left a pile of eggshells in the sink. As he spears the frittata with his fork, he fights back the urge to say, "You couldn't cook a real baby, India. A real baby would die."

That night as a peace offering, Uri rummages through the closet and finds a shoe box. He folds a couple of rags and then, in a particularly inspired moment, fills the rest with cotton balls. He sets the egg on top. It looks like it's floating on a cloud. He brings it to India while she's drinking tea in the study.

"Look," he says, setting the box by her keyboard. Her face goes blank.

"That's sweet," she says tentatively. "It's like a little bed."

"It *is* a little bed," Uri says. India nods.

In the bedroom, Uri sets the egg on the nightstand and waits for India to finish brushing her teeth. The egg's face is growing on him. The more he looks at it, the more he thinks he can see something sentient. A sparkle in the dried ink. A texture to the shell similar to the fine hairs on human skin. India comes in and takes off her yoga pants and top. She stands in front of the mirror looking at her body. Sometimes she turns and asks him if he thinks she's beautiful. It's amazing that she does this; she speaks with such derision about women (like her sister) who need constant affirmation. Tonight she doesn't ask him, though she scrutinizes her profile before grabbing her nightgown from the drawer.

She looks at the egg for a minute before she turns off the light.

"It looks like Groucho Marx," she says.

"It looks nothing like Groucho Marx," Uri says. "It doesn't have a mustache."

"Well, it looks like a weird old man," she says. Uri can smell her coconut face lotion and the rich unwashed oil of her hair. He thinks of Blithe. He thinks of pears.

Blithe trots down the maroon carpets of the office in a short wraparound dress. She's wearing sheer stockings and the same little black heels. She disappears into the file room and Uri imagines following, pushing her face first against the wall. She'd gasp and reach behind her to feel him, hard through his khakis.

Instead he goes into his office and flicks on the light, takes the egg, and sets it next to his phone. Then he thinks better of it and sticks it in his drawer.

He's halfway back to Berkeley that evening when he

realizes he's left it there. Rather than face India's wrath ("You left it at work? Imagine what would happen if you forgot a *baby*?"), he gets off the train in Oakland and takes another train back to the city. He sits next to an elderly Chinese woman clacking her dentures sloppily. As he disembarks, she takes out the teeth and stares at them as though a stranger left them in her mouth.

The security guard buzzes him in. It's nearly six o'clock and all the government workers have fled. The building is strangely muted. When he presses the door code he's met with the reassuring smell of reams of paper and printer toner. He's never thought of coming here to relax, but it's nice. Orderly.

"Oh," says Blithe. "I thought you'd gone." He's in his office, egg in hand. He quickly slips the egg into his trouser pocket. It bulges. He tries to dangle his hand in such a way that she won't notice. Her hair is falling out of her clips; she's distracted.

"I was just stood up," Blithe says. "It's the second time this guy's stood me up, and it's my birthday."

"Oh. That sucks," Uri says. Blithe stands there, looking miserable. "Happy birthday."

"Yeah, right."

Uri's heard Blithe complain about how much harder it is to make friends out west. No one's reliable and no one knows how to drink. He guesses it's true. Most of his buddies are from elsewhere: New York, Louisiana. India's from Detroit. Blithe looks like she's going to cry. India works late on Thursday nights and then she has a meditation class until half past nine.

"I can take you for a beer," Uri says. Blithe looks grateful.

They take the train to the Mission. Blithe knows a new tapas bar and they get a table near the window. Outside, a young woman with layered hair is unraveling a scarf as she yells into a cell phone. Next to her, two elderly women close up shop. They bring in a table of mangoes and plantains.

Blithe's face is so expressive. When she mimics her father's new girlfriend, a cattle dealer he met online, she expands her nostrils, widens her eyes, and talks without moving her tongue. Apparently, the woman has some kind of speech impediment. After two drinks, Uri's told her about growing up in Providence, his rocky relationship with his brother, Alvin, Alvin's ridiculous trophy wife, Bev (who *insists* on wiping down restaurant seats with disinfectant before she'll sit). Blithe laughs easily.

After the third round of drinks, Blithe leans close. She tells him her apartment is just around the corner, he should come see the watercolor her father sent for her birthday.

He shouldn't go. It's obvious where this is headed. He looks at his watch. It's eight. If he swings by, gets her home safely, he can make it back to Berkeley before India's class gets out. They leave the restaurant and he's careful to hold his bag over the bulge in his pocket. As they walk, her hand brushes his forearm twice and lingers. He breathes in sharply, getting a dizzying whiff of that pear shampoo.

Blithe's studio is IKEA tidy. Everything has a little red cabinet of its own. Her bed sits stately in the middle of the room, heaped with throw pillows in rich, dark colors. She has a little lamp with a beaded shade that throws gold light all over the covers. There's no other place to sit. Blithe goes to the little kitchenette, takes out an open bottle of bourbon, and pours them each a glass. Her squat, square tum-

blers have little Georgia peaches etched into them. She gestures to the painting on her bookshelf.

"I like the red in it," he says.

She faces him. They haven't had dinner and they're
both sufficiently drunk. Uri takes a big swallow. The bourbon's terrible—cheap with a sharp burn—but there's a nice
numb heat spreading over his chin.

"I've had so much fun with you tonight," Blithe says.
Her mouth is open slightly; her teeth look strong and clean.
"You've made my birthday."

Blithe waits, but Uri doesn't say anything. And then
she smiles slyly, reaches for the tie at her hip, and undoes
it. The dress falls open. Only the lace on her bra is black.
The rest is a rich, silken cream. Uri takes her by the waist
and pulls her toward him, sliding the dress off her arms
with his palms. Then it's like watching a tree fall in slow
motion: she barely bends, just falls on top of him, willingly,
sloppily, and as she lands Uri feels a crunch against his
thigh; wetness starts to ooze.

"Oh for Christ's sake," he says, pushing Blithe off him.
All the gold shards of light on the sheets are just India's
intelligent eyes, watching him silently as the egg makes its
way into his pubic hair.

Blithe gets another egg from the refrigerator, but she
doesn't have a Sharpie so he can't draw the face. And
what's more, there's a wet, sticky mess in his pants pocket
and all over the sock the egg was wrapped in. He rinses
both things out in the sink—but how will he explain to
India that the egg is now faceless, when she clearly saw that
he'd drawn on it, and that the sock is sopping wet?

"I don't understand," Blithe says. "What's it for?" Blithe's breath smells like Lysol.

"It's a competition," Uri says. He wants to say *with my wife,* but he's too much of a coward. Blithe must know he's married, though he's managed never to bring it up. He doesn't wear a ring. Neither does India. When they got married, India begged that they each tattoo a circle on their big toe. She thought it was more binding, not to mention more interesting. At that point in her life she was really caught up with being interesting.

Blithe's standing in the kitchen in only her bra and panties, the replacement egg held up like she's about to sing a jingle. She looks confused and he feels doubly guilty— for being with Blithe in the first place, and then for letting her down.

"I need another sock," Uri says. Blithe sets the egg on the counter and goes to find one.

It's not that late, only eight-forty, when he leaves Blithe's apartment, the new egg wrapped in Blithe's nicest sock. He left the pink one there, drying on the faucet. Down the street he finds a drugstore and buys a Sharpie. Carefully, on the way home, he re-creates the face he drew. The little eyes, the horseshoe nose. He does a reasonable job.

"Where were you?" India says when he walks in.

"I went out for drinks," Uri says. He bangs his leg on the trunk by the front door and when he leans down to rub it, he stumbles and catches himself on the molding.

"Are you drunk?" India asks.

"I guess, a little."

"Who were you with?"

"Just Tom. And this new investigator." He rubs his leg

until he can feel a heat there, then takes the egg out from his bag and sets it on top of the trunk. His jacket covers the wet spot on his pants.

"I got the egg a new outfit," he says before she can notice. The sock he took from Blithe is cashmere—she made sure to tell him this as she dangled it in front of him—light cream with little blobs of blue in it.

"Where'd you get a sock?" India asks, coming over to take a look.

"I bought it at lunch."

"What happened to the pink sock?"

"The egg didn't like it."

"The egg didn't like it?" India says, lowering one eyebrow. She looks like she's about to push the issue, but decides to let it go. She runs her thumb and forefinger around the edge.

"It's cashmere," Uri says.

"I don't have any socks this nice," India says. "Lucky egg."

In the morning, India brings him coffee and toast in bed. "Why the special treatment?" he asks.

"I want to talk to you," she says, and immediately, her eyes tear. Uri feels his gut flip. How could she know? He reaches for her hand; her bones are thin under her warm skin. He has an urge to take this hand and squeeze, feel the bones bend and snap. His hangover threatens to drag his tongue back down inside of his body and disintegrate it. India stares out the window by the bed and Uri looks out too. Two squirrels squabble on the fence.

"I was trying to figure out what my deal is," she says.

"And I think I'm just really afraid that I won't be a good enough parent."

Uri relaxes. It's nothing he hasn't heard before. India's mother is an alcoholic. When India was thirteen, her mother, in the middle of a rant about how India would soon be off "participating" with men, put on an Aerosmith record and cut off her own ponytail. The next day, instead of apologizing for the theatrics, she volunteered to show India how to make paintbrushes out of it. He pulls India toward him.

"You'll be fine," he says because it's true, but also because that's his script; there's nothing else he can say.

"I just called the doctor. If you're sure it's what you want," she says into his shoulder, "I'll get the IUD removed today. They can fit me into a cancellation at four." Uri nods and they make a quick plan: he'll get off at three and meet her there. His heart beats in his chin and wrists and groin and he takes India's hair, lifts it up so that her head rises with it and she starts to object, then presses her down beside him on the bed. He studies her face. She's striking, not just pretty like Blithe. Her hair is black and her eyes are a pale, frigid gray. She broke her front tooth in a car accident when she was twenty and the dentist smoothed the jagged edge. When they first began living together he would look at her offhandedly when he was watching television and the sight of her, all weird angles and paint-smeared jeans, would send a watery rush through him. He rests his head on her chest for a while, then gets up to take a shower.

He comes back to the bedroom to pick up the egg.

"You don't have to do that anymore," she says. But he finds that he wants the egg with him.

On the train, Uri shuts his eyes and focuses on a shape. It's something India does that he thinks is dopey, but it seems to work for her. He picks a circle. Once it's lodged in his mind, he tries to let his thoughts fall away. Then he asks himself how he's feeling. The circle is black, then it slowly turns silver. It bends into a sperm shape, then bends back. The train's crowded; Uri's holding onto the rail. He's bad at meditating. At the next stop, a very pregnant woman gets on and a young man stands to let her sit. The woman glances at Uri and gives him a bland smile. He turns away and imagines her standing up, a big puddle of water forming beneath her. The nasal sound of her bleating in pain. He imagines the way she will smell as her insides start to come out—blood, mucus, chains of membrane—and the coffee he drank on an empty stomach sloshes miserably.

Blithe is wearing a dark pantsuit and somber barrettes; Uri takes this as a sign that she has an investigation out of the office. He's right. She comes by at nine-thirty to tell him she's going to Fairfield to look into a race complaint at the city's sanitation facility.

"Did you work out the egg thing?" she asks.

"Yeah, it's all fine," he says. She bites her top lip and taps a finger on his door frame.

"Can I come in for a sec?" she asks. She closes the door behind her. "I just wanted to check in with you about last night. I mean, it seemed like you left in a rush, and—well, I guess I like you and I just—I didn't mean to freak you out."

It's absurd to see her in a suit now that he's seen her almost naked. It's a little like her satin bra and panty set are etched on top of the blazer and trousers. A panty phantasm. And what's more, the older she tries to dress, the younger she looks.

"Blithe, I'm married," he says. She looks briefly stunned.

"Oh God," she says slowly. "I'm a horrendous idiot."

"No," he says. "No one's an idiot." Blithe puts her hand on the doorknob. "Can we be friends?" he says, giving her the hangdog, boyish look he hasn't given anyone in years. The words linger around the office like a fart and Blithe looks at him coolly. She opens the door and leaves.

The miserable attorney calls again to screech about money. Uri says he's sorry, but he thinks he's coming down with the flu and needs to reschedule.

Three o'clock comes slowly. It has taken all his energy not to call India's cell phone to tell her to forgo the appointment. He tells himself that they still have a ways to go; she's not pregnant yet and if it's not meant to be then she won't get pregnant and they can maybe get another egg or a dog or just volunteer at a preschool.

The trains are delayed and India is already in the examining room when he gets there. The receptionist, a pear-shaped woman with thinning hair, takes him to her. India's got a piece of waxy paper draped over her lower half. She's on her back on the table with her feet in stirrups. He has the egg box with him and he sets it down on top of India's folded clothes. Before he can say anything, the nurse raps on the door and enters. She's tiny with a severe hairdo.

"I'm Nurse Practitioner Wu," she says to India. "I just need you to relax and scoot up on the table a little bit." Nurse Practitioner Wu snaps on latex gloves, gets out a tube of KY, and smears some on the metal speculum.

It's a quick procedure—a tug and a yelp.

"That's that," India says. Her face is pale. Uri smooths back her hair.

It's all happening a little fast, this bright road to fertility. Uri still feels fragile from drinking too much last night, but he buys a six-pack of beer on the way home. Sitting at the kitchen table, he opens one and gazes at the egg in its box. It smiles stiffly. India comes in and grabs a beer. She straddles a chair and sits on it backward, resting her chin on the high wooden back. She tosses the bottle cap onto the table, then reaches out and touches Uri's cheek. She's going to try to seduce him. She's pursing her lips. How can she not have noticed that the egg is different? When Uri looks at it, he can tell. He can see that the nose is way bigger than the nose he originally drew. The smile is wiggly, too. And what's more, the old egg was a small egg and Blithe's eggs were jumbo. This is a jumbo egg with a crooked smile and India is not noticing. She gets up off the chair and tilts her head back to take a swig of beer. She hiccups and then tosses herself in his lap, pressing her cold nose against his jaw. He slides his hand under her shirt for a minute, lets her start to kiss the side of his head.

"I'm not into it right now," he says, moving his legs so she's not as close to him. India stops.

"All right," she says, but it's a hurt all right.

He stays in the kitchen, working his way through the six-pack. He rolls the egg over. No little red mouth. That egg is gone. He's tired from drinking, from Blithe's rebuff, from the knowledge that he will have to go to work every day now in a state of semi-shame. And that's not all. From the lawyer's screaming, from the sight of India in stirrups, from the hurt way she walked out on him a half hour ago.

There's no way he can go through with it. She was right; he's ruined the barbecue and he's ruined the egg and he's basically ruined his whole goddamned life.

He goes out to the back deck and looks at the sky. It's late fall and the days have gotten shorter. The backyard is becoming shadow and silhouette, navy and gray. The long leaves of the eucalyptus tree shudder. He brings the egg to his nose; it smells like Freon and plastic, like the inside of a refrigerator. He aims it at the eucalyptus and misses. The egg falls to the ground and cracks.

Uri thinks of a farm out where his family used to vacation. The angry, cold eyes of the chickens kept there, the dank smell of bird shit in soil. He and Alvin used to swim in a nearby quarry. When they were old enough, they'd borrow his dad's truck and speed down dirt roads. The dust streaked Uri's skin and made his hair coarse. He thinks of Alvin running and plunging into bottomless gunmetal water. The way he would cry out, the splash and then the silence.

India comes onto the porch.

"What's going on?" she asks, touching his back. She follows his gaze to the egg. He turns to her, ready to plead—for what, he's not quite sure—when he sees that she's laughing. "Oops," she says. Her dark lashes shine in the last light of dusk.

THE TILT

I'T'S DAY TWO OF OUR FIVE-DAY VISIT TO MAINE AND Nick's stepmother, Anna, has barely uttered a word to us. She sits in the center of the braided rug in lotus position, her body draped in a faded violet sweat suit. The room used to hold a giant loom, but it's been moved to the garage. Now the room is empty save for a few low benches where candles burn and bundles of leaves sit, wrapped in embroidery floss.

"Just ignore her," Nick says. I follow him up the shiny wooden staircase to the bedrooms. He's not ignoring her. He's learned to live with all of this silently, but if I reached out to put my hand on his shoulder right now, he would feel as tense as a snake drawing back to bite.

The whole scene is wrong. It's been wrong from the beginning. When Nick was twelve and his father, Gray, left his mother for Anna—that was wrong. It was wrong that Nick's mother had to live alone in that run-down rental on the outskirts of town, drowning the noise of the neighbors with her radio, while Gray and Anna woke to views of rolling hills. The world has continued to spin like this, tilted poorly on its axis, and it's worn a lopsided groove in the universe.

Despite the sun streaming through the skylights and the white, clean walls, there's no peace here. The door to Milo's bedroom is shut, but I know that if we opened it, the bed would be unmade, the snowboarding poster would still hang on the wall above it. Anna will not allow the room to be emptied or cleaned; it's a battle she's been winning for years.

The windows in Nick's room open to the garden. The air is cool, spring, eastern wood air—the sweet smell of old leaves and new buds. It's a tiny room. There's hardly anything in here—an antique dresser with an old porcelain pitcher on it and a stiff-backed chair next to the bed. No trace of Nick as a child. Milo, age seven or eight, grins from a speckled silver frame. On the wall hangs a framed crayon drawing—Milo's, certainly.

"What do you want to do today?" Nick asks. He wriggles out of his thick brown sweater. It's not really warm enough to be without a sweater, but I admire his optimism. The trees outside shine in the brightness of the day. In the distance, you can hear the bleating of the sheep, occasionally, the squawk of a chicken.

Nick and I used to come up to this big house on long weekends, but I haven't been back in the three years since Milo's funeral. That day, we came up to this room, climbed into bed, blind with shock and exhaustion, and Nick told me that someday he would really understand love, but that he didn't think he did then, he didn't think he ever really had—at least not with me. Under the thick quilt his body altered, became solid and separate in a way I hadn't known before. His knees were sharp, his legs selfish. Inside my own body—which was already still with grief—a deeper silence landed. I closed my eyes and the darkness was particulate, full of spinning shards and gyrating orbs, but my blood and heart had stopped moving.

Nick waits for me to say something. He leans against the dresser, crossing his arms. His eyes are the impossible green of old Coke bottles and shine with a cool, glassy clarity. I could walk across the room and put my lips against his neck and he would put his hand on my back absently and I would stand there breathing the soapy smell of his skin.

The mattress sags when Nick sits. We've only been back together six months. Nick got a job in San Francisco, heading the archival sound department at the public library. He called me once he took the job. We met in Golden Gate Park, went to a bar, then back to his apartment with the futon on the floor and his clothes in low crates. We drank hot toddies and I wouldn't let him touch me. "I'm so sorry," he said. "You have to believe me." And I haven't forgotten about the way he left me, the girls he plugged the absence with until I didn't want to talk to him anymore, until whatever passed between us just felt like a joke, some adolescent clinging we never should have engaged in.

"How long does Anna do that for?" I ask. Nick sits up straighter.

"Oh, Becca," he says, putting a hand over his eyes. "Let's not get into this now."

"We're not getting into anything. I'm just asking a question."

"This isn't the worst of it," he says. "There's a group

that comes on Sunday nights." Outside a car whizzes past on the main road with a horse trailer. A bunch of geese rise off the small pond and disappear over the house. "They channel the dead," he says. He turns to face me, smirking. Does he really think I can't see it—the broken look that's particular to this older Nick? A mild shifting in the facial muscles that might be mistaken for aging?

"How many are in the group?"

Nick sighs. "I don't know, about five."

"They meet here?" I ask.

"Sometimes here, sometimes at other people's houses." He cracks the knuckles of his left hand. "Let's go get the bikes."

But on the way out to the shed, Nick's father, Gray, barrels up the driveway in his old pickup. He pulls up next to us.

"Becky!" he shouts. Nick kicks the gravel behind me. Gray's been on call since we arrived, so this is the first time I've seen him. He swings himself down from the cab; he's dressed in scrubs and white running shoes. Some of his neck hairs scraggle up around the vee of the shirt. He looks older, as if he's worn a hole in his body somewhere and the water in his skin has leaked out.

"Welcome!" he shouts. I'd forgotten how tightly wound he is. A dad on fast-forward. He talks as if someone's put a time constraint on his life. "It's been too long! Too long!" He thumps me on the arm, then grabs it and pulls me into an awkward hug. He smells strange, like the inside of a film canister.

"You always were a pretty one," he says, winking at Nick. Nick grimaces. "What are you two up to?"

"We're going to the reservoir," Nick says, and I can feel

his body gravitating toward the shed. Part of him is already on that bike, fleeing down the gravel road.

"Oh, no. Come inside and we'll make a pot of coffee. Becky, I want to hear how you're doing—Becky, Becky." He shakes his head. "And Nick, I was hoping you could pull up some chairs from the basement for dinner tonight."

"Dinner?" Nick asks.

"Anna invited some people over." Nick tenses. I step backward into him, but he doesn't soften or put his hand on me. Gray fishes a bag out of the bed of the truck. He swats me on the arm again as he walks into the house.

While Gray makes coffee, Nick and I go down to the basement to find the folding chairs. They're under a bunch of tarps and old paint cans, and Nick begins to dig them out.

"You okay?" I ask. His hair falls over his eyes.

"Mmm," he says. "He put this damn belt thing over the chairs. Why would you do that?" Nick yanks on the belt and the chairs, which sit on wheeled palettes, roll toward him slightly. "It's like he's afraid even the fucking chairs are going to try to get out of here." Nick kneels over the strap and starts to wiggle the metal clasp. I hoist myself up to sit on a workbench. Above my head the shelves are stocked with Ball jars of pickles and jams. The three freezers whir and hum. I like it down here. It's organized and spotless, and there's a feeling of abundance. At Thanksgiving, every dish Gray and Anna serve they've grown and prepared themselves, including the turkey. There's something romantic about it, even if it is self-righteous, as Nick says.

Nick gets the belt off and the chair on the end falls to the ground, making a sharp clatter.

"Take two of them," Nick says, grabbing three more off the end. The wooden stairs creak as we head back up.

"Thanks, kids," Gray says. He's holding a black plastic pitcher of coffee and three mugs. Anna still sits cross-legged on the small carpet in the weaving room, her eyes closed, her spine rigid. Gray doesn't acknowledge her.

You wouldn't know it was Anna who planned the dinner. She's still very quiet, even after the guests arrive, and she's careful to sit next to Gray at the corner of the table. She was young when she married him, twenty-six to his forty-one. Her face is still smooth, despite the hollowing of her eyes. She's done something odd with her hair tonight, a princess Leia look with braided buns muffling her ears.

"I lost my baby," the woman next to me says. I can't remember her name. She holds her knife and fork above her plate and trembles slightly. Her bright blond hair is pinned loosely on top of her head so that it flops to one side and her gray eyes are as focused as a gun. She's shockingly pretty. The smattering of color in her cheeks looks like a small, ragged continent. "He was only six months old," she says. The rest of the guests talk loudly about Gray and Anna's recent kayaking trip.

"I'm so sorry," I say.

"And then I lost my husband," she says. "To leukemia last year." I can't bring my knife down to the chicken on my plate, though I want to. A gesture of normalcy, cutting chicken off the bone. Nick hasn't touched his food. I can tell he's listening to the blond woman, but he doesn't turn to help me out. He just grabs his bottle of beer and takes a purposeful swig. I set my knife down.

A peal of laughter erupts from the head of the table.

"That's terrible," I say.

"It changes you," she says. Nick picks up the bowl of green beans.

"You want some?" he asks, handing it over to me. I take the bowl and hold it for a moment. It feels heavier than it should. I'm afraid I'm going to drop it.

"Thanks," I mumble. I set it between the blond woman and me. The beans look oily. I can't think. If I don't leave, I feel like I might pass out.

"I have to go to the bathroom," I say, scooting my chair out. "I'm sorry." It's awful to do this, to let her words hang in the empty air over my place setting, but I don't have it in me to respond. I don't even know what a response would sound like.

In the bathroom, I sit on the lid of the toilet and focus on my breathing. It's cold in here. Nick and I spent the afternoon helping out around the garden, drinking beer after beer, and then Scotch as we roasted the chicken with Gray, then more Scotch as we hovered around the crackers with the guests as they filtered in. I'm feeling less drunk than tired. Tired from the roof of my mouth inward, into the pockets behind my eyes, down in my windpipe and deep in my lungs.

We've talked about death, Nick and I. It's like a secret we pass around at night but don't dare mention in the light of day. Three years ago, Milo took a rifle out of the gun cabinet and went outside to shoot at the geese. He was fourteen years old. When Anna came home with a pizza from town, Milo was facedown on the grass in a pool of blood.

The day of Milo's funeral I locked myself in this bathroom and cried until I was sick. I imagined Milo crinkling to the grass after the bullet went smashing through his temple. I imagined the bits of gray brain that wormed their way between the green blades, the dark black of his blood, the hose the medics used to wash it away, how his skin sank to his bones moments later. I'd been at the house a few months before and Milo would spend all day in the game room obsessively playing pool by himself. His unwashed hair stuck to his forehead in serpentine clumps. He was small for his age, with long eyelashes and a thin neck.

"We'll show you how it's done," Nick told him, taking a cue down from the wall. But Milo shook his head. "I'm practicing," he said. "Alone." Every time we passed the game room, we could hear the clack of pool balls. We ignored him. It seemed to be what he wanted.

But what made me cry wasn't really Milo. It was the hole that Milo left that frightened me. My mother had been sick for nearly five years. Her death was in every absence— in the quiet of the air when the phone didn't ring, the emptiness of a white wall, the sleeping moments of the cat. It hung around my hands and hair like a fog.

The first year Nick and I dated, our freshman year of college, I lived in a dorm that used to be the women's infirmary, back when the women's college was separate from the men's. It still looked like a hospital, each room complete with a sink and cold slate floors. The building was U-shaped and when the winds picked up in winter, they'd shriek against the stone. I had fevers that year, fevers and hives for no reason anyone could detect. And Nick sat up with me boiling water in the electric kettle, making me powdered soups and tea. He joked about the ghosts of the dead girls and made weird hoo-ing sounds before I'd fall asleep. In my fever dreams, they would appear, the dead girls, their cheeks sanguine, their eyes sad. They'd be dressed in plain cotton gowns and they would show me their hands, always too small for their bodies.

I put my hand on the porcelain sink beside me. It's solid and cool and real, and I wish I could carry it out with me, sit it beside the table. I have to get back to the dinner. Nick isn't going to come to find me, though I wish he would. I wish he would come down the hall and knock on the door and make hoo-ing sounds.

Nick still hasn't touched his food. The blond woman talks with the two women on her right. She doesn't turn to face me as I slip back into my chair. I put my hand on Nick's leg under the table. He gives me a sideways glance.

"We haven't seen Becky in years," I can hear Gray saying.

"Becca," Anna says.

"What?"

"It's Becca, Gray." Gray shrugs and leans closer to the bearded man. He sits on the opposite side of Anna and she leans away from Gray as he moves over her. "I think we've got a wedding in the future." He's drunk. Nick breathes in sharply and grabs at the beer again. I take my hand back.

After Milo's funeral, Gray collapsed in my lap on the sofa and sobbed. *I love you,* he kept repeating. *Never stop telling your mother that, Becca. Never stop telling your family how much you love them.* When I told Nick, he was mortified.

After dinner, Gray suggests that we all go for a walk. There's a trail that leads out near the pond, into the woods beyond, up a small ridge to a clearing. Nick and I spent many hours one summer with hoes and weed clippers, clearing that trail.

There's polite talking as the guests get their coats on. The blond woman isn't really dressed for a hike. She wears red clogs and a long camel-colored coat. I wonder if she's new to these parts, if she came out here to forget. She's not doing a good job, if that's the case.

There are five guests. Two of the women have permed helmets of brown curls. One is tall and buxom, the other is short and slight, but they both wear boxy wool blazers and simple neutral pants with shoes that resemble brown bricks. And there's the angular wife of the bearded man who keeps nervously reaching out to touch him as though he might vanish. Nick smooths my hair back, yanks on a handful until I'm turned to face him, then he leans down and puts his nose against my jaw.

Everyone else waits outside. Their voices are getting less defined as they walk down the lawn to the start of the trail.

"Sorry about this," Nick says.

"About what?"

"About what," he says, shaking his head. "Right."

I can choose. He might be sorry about bringing me here, into this wound of family that can't seem to heal. He might be sorry for Gray's drunkenness, for Anna's silence, for the blond woman's confession, for the fact that we'll have to spend the evening in the woods with five strangers. He might just be sorry. Sorry for leaving me when he did, sorry for returning with streamers of pain rustling behind him, sorry for my mother's descent, for the fact that once she's gone, I will be without family. Sorry for the tilted world. Or simply sorry for himself.

We trail along behind the group and Nick takes my hand as we pass the pond. How long did it take Gray and Anna before they could come out here again? Before they stopped seeing Milo on the grass, Milo against the sky, Milo in all the geese flying by? Or do they still see him, feel him in the night breeze, see his thin, gangly frame scurrying out in the distance, playfully dodging them?

I move my thumb over Nick's thumb and feel a wash of tenderness.

The group has fallen silent. The wind blows through the boughs of the pine trees, rushes over the pond. Even the animals are quiet in the barn down the driveway.

There are a couple of benches by the pond, before the start of the trail, and Nick pulls me over to one. We sit close together. Behind us, the group continues to walk. Soon they'll be in darkness, the woods lit only by Gray's old headlamp.

I didn't see her hang back.

"Can I sit?" Anna asks.

"Of course," I say, gesturing to the spot beside me.

She closes her coat around her and hunches into it, sinks to the bench. The group's footsteps disappear into the woods.

"How's your mother doing, Becca?" she asks. I have stock responses to this question, depending on who asks it. Status quo, not well, very bad. No one ever really wants to hear about it, and so I try to keep the answers short. She's dying. I could say this. Though they cut off her breasts, though her diaphragm is paralyzed from radiation and she can't breathe without tubes, she's still here. She still makes jokes about the dog and gets angry with the doctors. She can't figure out how to use her cell phone or get the stains out of the grout in the kitchen. But when I touch her skin, the heat is different. Defeat and fury lie right below the coolness of it. A frightening combination—defeat that

won't do you in and fury that can't save you. And sometimes I try to imagine the silence that will fall everywhere
after she dies. I call her now with an offhanded question
about taxes or recipes and I think that soon there will be no
answers. And the question mark will lose its curve, will
grow and straighten inside of my ribs, getting so large and
sharp that it finally splits my body in two.

"She's hanging in there," I say. Anna nods. We don't
look at each other.

"Give her my love," Anna says.

Only the whisper of wind through trees, only the distant throaty singing of frogs.

"Do you want to walk, Bec?" Nick's voice is loud.
Anna stands and takes a flashlight out of her jacket pocket.
She twists the head of it until a dim nickel of light lands on
the dirt.

She gestures with her head. "We should catch up."

Nick walks quickly, gets ahead of us, and then stops
near the trees to wait.

There's something between Anna and me right now,
something warm and desperate and sad. I want to ask her
what she hears when Milo comes to her, when he materi-
alizes out of wind and light. Does he simply sit near her?
Is it like she's pregnant with him again? Does he get
lonely? Does he tell her why he did it? How the gun felt?
What that moment was like when his finger tightened
around the trigger? Did he think about Anna, the pow-
dery smell of her neck, the drugged feeling of sleeping near
her when he was small? Was it brilliant, that smash of
pain? Did he see colors? Did he feel love and sorrow surge
up in his throat and go soaring out of him? Was that what
death was? No longer needing to contain these feelings in

your body? When suddenly, all the splitting song inside you *is* you. You are—finally—no longer a container—you are the things that once were contained?

Anna tried to kill herself a month after it happened. She took sleeping pills and locked herself in the bedroom. She took too many, though, and just threw them up. "I want to go with him," she screamed at Gray, or so the story goes. She screamed this over and over until Gray loaded her up in the truck, took her to the emergency room, and had her sedated.

Anna's flashlight shines uselessly on pieces of earth and rock. We walk through the woods mostly by instinct. I reach out and grasp Nick's arm. He squeezes my hand between his arm and chest.

When we get to the top of the ridge, I can see the group at the far corner. Gray has a thermos and passes it between himself and the bearded man. The two permed women stand close together. The blond sits alone on a rock overlooking the property. Her chin rests on her knees.

Did the angular woman and bearded man have a child die, too? Were we all going to sit on top of this ridge and hum? Would the dead come floating off the tips of trees, would the girls come back in their cotton gowns, would their shrunken hands scratch at my face?

A buzzing begins in my head. I want to go tearing off down the path, across Maine, across this enormous country, back to that other ocean. But I just stand there, staring out into the night, Nick's arm clamping my hand to his side. Anna walks over to the blond woman and sits beside her. Their bodies are darker and more substantial than night, and I can see Anna's pale hand settle on the woman's neck. The woman bends toward her.

Maybe it's not Milo's return that Anna's seeking. Maybe she just wants the world to stop spinning for a moment. Maybe she's looking for stillness, a place where the questions don't haunt her, where Milo is actually gone.

At the end of the clearing, Gray laughs at something the bearded man says. Nick takes my hand in his and pulls me toward them.

THE BEADS

WHEN MY FATHER FIRST SUGGESTED SHE DONATE her body to research, my mother stared at him like he'd just grown a beak. Eventually, though, she relented. "It's not like it'll do me much good when I'm dead, dear," she said to me, signing her name with a flourish. She straightened the edges of the forms with the flat of her palm and settled down to watch a movie. We never discussed her decision again.

About two weeks after her death, my father called me at home.

"Yael, I've got some strange news." He was using his doctor voice, clipped and clinical. "I just got a call from the lab." My heart soared. It wasn't my mother who died! (I knew it!) The whole thing had been a bizarre mix-up—somebody else's mother. My mother was alive, sitting on a park bench in Boise eating cherries!

"They've done some work on her cadaver." My soaring halted. "It seems that your mother's stomach was full of beads."

"Beads?"

"Yes," he said. "Very strange."

When my mom went into the hospital for what we knew would be the final time, my father packed his bags. He'd rented a furnished apartment in the foothills. "A blank slate," he'd said as he showed me the empty cupboards. The apartment belonged to a large, beige development over-looking a man-made pond. I drove through the mechani-cal gates and found him pacing outside his front door. On the dining room table in a gallon zipper bag, the beads waited. They ranged in size. Some were like large pearls while others resembled popcorn kernels. And they ranged in color, too—blues, glossy green, bloody scarlet, others like bone or dirty stucco. I lifted a fistful and a few fell to the carpet. If my mother's skin had been translucent, she would have looked like a cathedral window.

My father breezed behind me on the way to the kitchen. "I'm having a Scotch," he said. "You want one?" We sat on the living room floor with the beads beside us, sipping from the tumblers in silence.

I couldn't remember my mother ever wearing beads. She'd been raised in Brooklyn and despite my parents' migration to California in the 1970s, she'd never gotten hip to the bohemian thing. She liked gold jewelry. Classy little hoops hooked into her ears. A delicate gold band on her ring finger.

My mother was a woman devoid of fancy. She felt no remorse as she threw out my childhood paintings or my father's love letters. She bought tuna fish on sale and bulk flour. Were these beads her private code? Did she secretly long for color and excess? Did one bloom each time she fingered a silk scarf or expensive underwear? Or did the beads have to do with her disease? For every cell that went astray, her body produced a bead as an apology.

Finally, my father spoke. "She must have eaten them," he said.

My father was a doctor and so the world revealed itself to him in an orderly fashion. There were things that were possible and things that were not. I reached out for a green bead and held it to the light.

"Why would she have done that?" I asked.

"We'll never know," he said gravely.

I knew this was absurd. My mother disliked all things strange. She was a finicky eater and she'd been in the hospital for weeks before she died. Who would have fed her beads?

"I'm getting rid of them," he said.

"No," I said. "I'll hold on to them." My father nodded absently and rubbed the back of his neck.

When I got home, I rinsed them off and put them in a metal mixing bowl in my bathroom. My boyfriend, Mateo, stood over them and twirled a piece of his hair, something he did when he puzzled over crosswords or talked to a difficult editor on the phone.

"It's got to be a sick joke," he said, walking back into my bedroom. He sat on the bed. "That's just too messed up."

"A joke?" I asked.

"I don't know. Maybe there's some sort of pathology lab fraternity brotherhood or something."

I got off the bed.

"What?" he said. "You think all those beads just magically appeared inside your mother?"

I walked into the bathroom, locked the door, turned off the light, and shoved my hand deep into the bowl. The knobby pressure on my fingers felt good—like shoving my hands into river gravel. If there were enough of them to fill the bathtub, I'd have slept in them.

"Yael?" Mateo called.

I took a bead between my thumb and forefinger. I could make out, though the room was dark, a slight red sheen. I slipped it into my mouth and swallowed.

"Please open the door," Mateo said, his voice grave, authoritative.

I unlocked it. The hair Mateo tugged stuck from his head like a frosting dollop and he had a piece of lint on his eyebrow. "Come here," he said. He'd just shaved, and he smelled very strongly of lemons. *My mother is dead,* I said to myself. But the words sounded ridiculous. *Mateo is being nice to me because my mother is dead.* I pushed him aside and climbed into bed.

"I'm exhausted," I said. But really, I just wanted to close my eyes. I wanted to see if I could feel it, that shiny red bead, slipping silently through me.

When the alarm went off, I woke feeling strangely elated.

"Teo," I whispered. I could tell he was awake. I shoved my foot between his ankles and felt his scratchy leg hairs. "Wake up." I ran a hand down his chest, hooked a finger in the elastic of his boxers, scooted close. He opened one eye.

"What time is it?" He lifted his head to look at the clock and groaned. "I have that meeting at eight-thirty," he said. "Those sadists."

Mateo and I left each other alone in the mornings. We both hated the violence of waking, hated each and every bird that chirped. But this morning the sun was coming right out of the center of my stomach. Mateo made a move to get out of bed, but I crooked my arm around his neck. I felt radiant, zinging with life.

"Are you okay?" he asked.

"Yes," I said, rolling on top of him. "I'm good." I began to tug off his T-shirt.

After he left, vaguely puzzled and disheveled, I carried the bowl of beads to the coffee table. I gathered the necessary materials: dental floss, scissors, a sewing needle. The beads gathered on the string, and when it was long enough, I tied it off. It hit just over my heart.

I'd forgotten about it by the time Mateo got home. He came into the house, set his bag down, and headed to the kitchen when he stopped short.

"You made a necklace?" I fingered the beads. Red, dirty stucco, blue.

"What?" I said.

Mateo shook his head and raised his arms a little, then dropped them to his sides. "Yael," he said, squinting a little. "That's just wrong."

"I think they're beautiful."

"Those beads," Mateo started, and then shook his head. His voice was a higher pitch than usual. "Those beads were sitting in your mother's stomach!" He waited for me to get it, to take the necklace off and hurl it to the carpet. I put my hand over the beads.

"Do you not see that that's disturbing?"

"You said you thought it was a joke," I said.

Mateo continued to shake his head. "I don't know how to deal with this." He stormed past me to the patio, where he sat stiffly, staring at a tree.

"Maybe it's too hard," he said. "Maybe I just can't take it." I sat on the deck chair beside him. "I don't know what you want from me. Are you punishing me for something?" In the dimming light of the summer sky the beads looked almost supernatural, like a wad of colored foil burned in the center of each one. "It's just so much pressure," he said. I looked out into the trees behind the house. It was nearly dusk and they cast long shadows over the lawn. I closed my eyes and a peaceful sensation drifted in, right where the necklace fell over my chest. It spread through my body like a vapor.

"Please take the beads off," Mateo said. I'd climbed in bed next to him in my nightgown. The beads hung beneath the thin fabric, making a ridge.

"No," I said. "They give me comfort." I hadn't expected to say this, but after I did, I realized it was true.

Mateo rolled onto his back and breathed deeply. "Don't I give you comfort?" he asked.

"Of course you give me comfort," I said. But it wasn't true. He rolled away from me.

I couldn't sleep. If they had found these beads in my mother's stomach, then wasn't it possible they'd find other things as well? Keys? Scrolls? Tiny mirrors? I crawled out of bed and went into the living room to call my father. He picked up on the first ring, sounding frightened.

"Sorry. I can't sleep," I said. He sighed.

"I can't sleep either," he said. "I've been feeling very odd."

"Odd how?" I asked.

"Don't throw the beads out," he said. "I think we

should keep them in the family." I could hear him tinkering with something on the other end; it sounded like he was playing with silverware. "Yael, actually, do you think I could come over and take a look at them?"

"Now?" I asked.

"If that's okay. I know it's late."

Twenty minutes later, my father knocked softly on the front door. Red tinged the whites of his eyes and in the corners, a yellow gel gathered. He grabbed my shoulders stiffly and pulled. I tried to lean into the embrace, but it put me off balance.

"I don't understand," he said. He sat, placed the bowl in front of him on the floor, and shoved his hairy hand into the remaining beads. The muscles in his jaw pulled back, but the rest of his face got very still. He rocked, grasping his upper arms, kneading the flesh as if looking for a good place to grip. Then he began to cry out. I'd never heard him cry and the noises were tentative and jagged.

Mateo padded out of the bedroom in his socks and boxers. He looked at me, alarmed. I looked at my father. I'd heard stories about this. Women threw themselves on the graves of their dead husbands, eyes rolled back, throats dilated. But I hadn't expected it from him. When my mother stopped breathing, he put his hand on her head, then pulled the sheet over her face. He called the attending nurse. He made sure the right papers were signed.

When my father quieted, I felt the small hairs on my neck and arms reorient. He hung his head, balled his hands into fists, and wept. I kneeled next to him. Mateo followed and kneeled next to me. I put my hand on my father's back. Mateo put his hand on my back. My father took some deep breaths.

"I'm sorry," he said. "I'm sorry."

I shook my head and patted his back.

"Don't be sorry," Mateo said. I brought out extra sheets and blankets and put my father to bed on the sofa.

Back in the bedroom, Mateo wanted to know how I was. There was a feigned sympathy in his eyes, but behind that, exhaustion.

"I don't know," I said. I fumbled for the necklace beneath my robe. Warm from my skin, the beads felt animal and alive, as if inside of each of them beat a fragile little heart.

When I woke up, my father was drinking coffee on the sofa. Mateo had left for work.

"I'm sorry about last night," my father said. There was a grayish tint to his skin and his sideburns were completely white. He used to look tall and brusque, always rushing away in dark polished shoes. Now he wilted in beige sneakers and jeans.

"Don't be," I said. I went and sat next to him. Momentarily, his eyes locked on my neck.

"I made plans to go sailing today." He changed his focus, staring deeply at the coffee in his cup. "I'm trying to get out of the house."

"That's good," I said. But my mind wasn't linking up to the present. I could feel only the beads.

"I'm going with a nurse from the hospital, but I just want you to know that it's not really a date." I looked at him, still staring at the coffee.

"It's not a date," I repeated.

"Of course not," he said. "How could it be a date?"

"How could it be a date?"

"How could it be?" he asked.

A date? It had occurred to me that this would happen someday, but not two weeks after her death. She'd been sick for years, dying for months, but her death was new. It was like a magic trick, of sorts: now you see Mom in the bed, now you see a bed!

"I can't believe this."

"What?"

"I can't believe you'd even think of dating right now."

"I just told you it isn't a date," he said.

"She just died!"

"Yael, this is hard for me," he said. "I know it's hard for you, too. But I need to do something. I need to get out. I can't spend my days locked in the house, feeling that I never knew how to be happy and now I never will."

Happy? Of course he wasn't happy. They'd been married thirty years and now she was dead. Why would he be happy? And that he'd never been happy? Happy was a word to be squished through the nose at birthday parties.

"There's a lot you don't know," he said. "Your mother and I were our own people, not just your parents."

"Please leave." I stood and walked toward the door. My father, cowed, set the coffee cup down on the table, picked up his coat, and walked toward me.

"I'm only trying to be honest," he said.

Last night, as he wailed, I'd wished for him to stop. But now I wanted to switch the flip, watch him howl and bawl every day for the rest of his life. We'd take each bead and recount a memory of my mother: the way she tapped a dish after she washed it; the way she organized and labeled our camping gear, cut dreadlocks off the dog—and as we talked, we'd drown in borderless, limitless grief. When we got to the last bead, we'd start again.

"Go be honest somewhere else," I said.

I was supposed to meet Mateo for lunch downtown, but I had no interest in walking to the train. I didn't want to see him, his clean-shaven jaw, well-meaning eyes. I only wanted to see him if his mother was dead. I'd start a club. Maybe even a commune. I'd surround myself with people who would promise never to say the word "happy." Who wouldn't use it or any of its synonyms. We'd be like an experimental French novel. We'd even ban the letters of happy.

The phone rang and the machine picked up. No one left a message.

"What," I said when it started up again. My sharpness dissolved into crying.

"Yael?" Mateo sounded concerned. "I don't suppose you're coming for lunch? I was going to suggest that Japanese place, but another time. I'll just come home. Are you okay?"

Okay? Was okay like happy?

The bathroom tiles felt cool and gluey under my bare feet. All the crying had made me feel a little high. As the water crashed from the faucet of the tub, I dumped in the beads. They gathered near the drain, a colorful smattering of glass, brighter once submerged.

I took off my nightgown and sat until the water grew cold around me, gazing at the light blue ceiling, the small crack that led from the window above the tub to the corner of the room.

The front door opened and slammed.

"Yael?" Mateo called, walking toward our bedroom. I shivered, but I didn't want to move. I rolled the beads under my feet and stared at the shower curtain. A small vine of orange mold started at the bottom. Rust spotted the metal at the top of the curtain rod.

"Hey," he said, coming into the bathroom. He sat on the toilet and peered at me. My eyes felt dry, the skin around them thin and tattered.

"How are you?"

"Never better," I said.

"Okay," he said. There it was again, that stupid, stupid word. He reached over and tucked a wet strand of hair behind my ear. His hand lingered there. I put my hand on his for a moment, then pushed it away.

"I brought you some food from that soul food place on the corner," he said.

I didn't want to look at him. The rust growths looked like starfish.

He sighed. "Yael, you gotta help me out here. I'm doing the best I can."

This was Mateo's burden? Was I supposed to comfort him?

"Screw off," I said.

"Oh, that's really nice. I bring you lunch while you're acting like a total psychopath, rolling around in your mother's stomach remnants, and you tell *me* to screw off. You screw off." He continued to sit on the toilet. Why didn't he just leave? My insides were made of lint and tiny red embers, a combustible combination of stillness and

fury. He ought to get out now and find himself a nice girl
with two functional parents and maybe a little dog to play
with in the park.

"I'm not getting out," I said.

Mateo looked down at his shoes. Brown leather loafers,
appropriate for a budding journalist. News shoes. The toes
were worn, the rubber soles curving a bit at the heels. He
stood, took the bag of food, and walked out of the bathroom.

I thought I'd hear him leave. I waited for the door to
slam, but it didn't. He went into the kitchen. I sank down
into the tub and submerged myself. But as my head went
under, I had to bend my knees and they stuck out of the
water. I sat back up, my head soaked, my knees cold, and
started to shake.

Mateo came in holding my old bathrobe and the beach
towel. "Get out," he said. His voice was gentle. I looked
at him.

"I'm not ready to get out," I said.

"Get out anyway."

An order. How exciting. No one had told me what to
do in months, since the doctor gave my mother her final
prognosis. Everyone just nodded when I spoke. If they did
ask things, they asked gently. I was an ominous force, a
person to be pleaded with. I grasped the porcelain lip of the
tub and raised myself out. My hipbones jutted like fins near
my sunken stomach. I stepped onto the bath mat and
Mateo wrapped the towel around me, held out the robe.

He'd set the food on a silver baking pan on the dresser.
A yellow flower from the yard leaned in a large water
glass. After I got in bed, he situated the tray between us as
if it were a small child. He took a rib and started eating,

careful not to look at me. The beads were alarmingly bright.

The phone rang.

"You get it," I said to Mateo. He reached across me for the receiver. I could hear my father's voice booming.

"Mateo? Why are you home so early? Is everything okay?"

I tugged on the necklace and the knot gave. The string slid across my jugular, then into the robe. "Shit."

Mateo put his hand over the receiver. "Do you want to talk to him?" I shook my head, reaching down into the robe to gather the strays. Most of them still hung on the thread. Mateo held the phone to my ear anyway.

"Yael," my father said. I didn't say anything. "What are you doing?" I was trying to figure out if any more beads were under my thigh.

"Resting," I said, standing up, grabbing the phone.

"You can't bring her back," he said.

"No, *you* can't bring her back," I said. Between my thumb and forefinger I squeezed a white bead.

"I'm not sure what you mean by that." My father faltered. I clamped down on the bead as hard as I could, pressing my skin into the tiny eyelash etchings that graced the bead's surface. And then, as if in desperation, as if the bead had nowhere else to go, it popped from my fingers and flung itself down the heating vent. I threw the phone on the bed and pulled up the vent, but the bead was gone.

Mateo picked up the phone and politely asked my father if we could call him back. He got the vacuum out of the hall closet.

"I seriously doubt we'll be able to suction it up," he said, plugging in the cord. The vacuum revved excitedly. Mateo lowered the hose down deep. Then we heard a pop and crunch and Mateo flipped the power switch off. I unlatched the door and took out the bag. Fishing through dust and fibers I located it, broken into small white pieces, like doll teeth.

"We can glue it," Mateo said, taking the pieces from me. Downstairs in the laundry room we found some craft glue. He smoothed it on the ceramic surface with a small paintbrush and I used my fingers as a clamp. Mateo left me there. Gradually the milky glue began to turn clear.

When the bead seemed dry enough, I made my way back upstairs to restring the necklace. Mateo put on headphones, opting to ignore me. I set the broken bead in the center, flanked with red ones. I imagined my mother's skin, the way it was once—very pale, with blue veins in the temples and light freckles on her nose and eyelids. She sat on a lawn chair next to me. I was eleven. She held a cherry stem in her strong teeth and eyed me as I showed her how to tie one in a knot. She attempted to follow my lead, her mouth circling like she was chewing cud. Finally she stuck out her tongue to admit failure and the mangled stem fell against her clavicle.

I looked at the glue, jagged in the cracks. "Come back," I said to it. The bead said nothing. Mateo bobbed his head to the music and paged through a magazine, and for this I was grateful. If he moved closer, put his arm around me, I would have had to admit that I understood she was dead— that no amount of piecing her together would change that. It would have been like she was there on the carpet, her arms close to her side, her mouth cracked open as if trying to let in that last breath of air.

A ROMANCE

Mrs. Capp didn't tell me we were having company this morning, but when the bell rings, she flies to the door as if she's been waiting all her life. The man's a bit of a hippie with long, wavy blond hair and an unkempt beard.

"Liza, this is Satan." She says his name with such assurance I can't be sure I've heard her correctly. She articulated the "Sate" part far better than the "tan" part—and given his looks, he might be named "Seat-Man" or "Slaton."

"S-A-T-A-N?" I ask. He nods. I nod back. Am I missing something? Mrs. Capp did tell me, a few days ago, that she met a man while browsing through the record store downtown. "Nice-looking," she said. "And very knowledgeable about percussive jazz." She mentioned she might have him over sometime. But she didn't warn me that he was coming *this* morning.

"Nice to meet you," I say. I'm still in my pajamas, reading the newspaper. In large, gothic font across the top of the front section are the words NINE DEAD IN BUS COLLISION.

Satan jams a thumb through the hammer loop of his painter's pants. He looks at the paper and I think I see his blue eyes twinkle, then he looks guiltily away.

A few months ago, Mrs. Capp placed an ad in the local paper looking for "a quiet and respectful female roommate with a low tolerance for untidiness and a high regard for manners." We didn't hit it off so well the day I met with her about the room, but since she didn't get many responses, I ended up moving in.

In the time that I've lived here, I've gone on one date, a blind date engineered by my sister, Kate. Phil was very nice, in a helpless kind of way. Kate knew him from college. He had thin blond hair and watery eyes that sat too far apart. After speaking each sentence, he'd pause, as if his words needed time to percolate through a fine sieve. But most of the things he said to me were easy to digest, like "I was born in Seattle." This sort of phrase wouldn't be in response to a question (such as "where were you born?"), but would serve as an awkward opener. I felt like I was supposed to do something special with Phil's silences; they seemed coded and livelier than his speech. Though I was curious about his manner, I didn't want to date him.

Mrs. Capp, however, has been out numerous times with numerous men, some of them quite young. One I recognized from my graduate program, a squinty young man, Kirk Williams. In class it seemed he was trying to see the projected lecture notes with his front teeth. I can't figure out where she meets these men because she doesn't go out much and when she does she wears unflattering pleated skirts and necklaces that hang down, accentuating a tired-looking bosom. I suspect she's one of those librarian types that men fantasize about. They seem prim, but get them in a dark room and va-voom, the buttons are flying.

Mrs. Capp was married once to a man named Sal. She's in her mid-forties now, a little overweight. Sal, I gather, was considerably older. He was a professor at the small school where she earned her master's degree. Two years ago he died of a stroke. Mrs. Capp speaks highly of him. She sighs at good meals and comments on how he would have loved the lamb, the potatoes, the flavor of the dry wine.

I get the sense, though, that she didn't really know him that well. The stories she tells don't seem specific. When I tell her about Kevin, my ex-boyfriend, I never say, "Oh, Kevin loved comedy films." Instead, I say that when he was a baby he was born with two thumbs on each hand. The doctors immediately cut off the extras and Kevin still felt sore that no one consulted him about it.

You might think that living with Mrs. Capp has damaged my ego. After all, I am young, slim, in my prime. I should be the one waltzing off in tight pants on Friday nights. The messages on the phone pad should be for me. But in truth, I didn't move here to meet people. I came here to retreat. At some point last year, I realized that I didn't like many of my friends in California. They were just people living boring lives that seemed less boring because they were young and busy. But each of them toiled away at meaningless jobs, showered with water from the same treatment facility, had the same hurt feelings when their lovers broke their hearts.

It's not that I fancied myself different from them. It was that I began to see myself as indistinguishable. Rachel

Klegman would order a turkey sandwich and I'd want the same thing. She'd buy new shoes and I'd have them already. Stacy Wong would fight with her father and come over crying and I'd realize that I'd had that fight with my own father. Instead of making me feel comforted, one of a great community of souls, I found myself trying to pump my experiences up so that they'd look unique. I'd embellish my trip to the drugstore. I told Kevin that I saw a brown ring of what looked like lipstick smudged onto the floor in the center of the feminine hygiene aisle. I said it looked like a sign, a secret message left by a fugitive. A symbol that he was whole, alive, well.

"They never clean that store," Kevin replied.

And I understood what I was doing. This took most of the fun out of it.

The East Coast began to look like frontier, the new world beckoning to me with its welcoming, deeply lined hands. It was the only way to extricate myself from the excruciating plainness of my life: Kevin, the jars of chutney crystallizing in the fridge, the relentless Friday-night parties where self-congratulatory med students and budding PhDs got drunk on gin and pretended to forget the rules of social interaction.

Now I am three thousand miles away, eating pasta and canned tomatoes and picking my toenails while I read. And watching Mrs. Capp fuss with her hair and apply too much rouge, I'm reminded that it's hell to care about the world the way that she does.

Satan lingers in the doorway, grinning. "Well, come *innn*," Mrs. Capp coos. For a moment he's frozen in the sunlight, and then, with a loping gait, he follows her into the kitchen.

I should have known that she was up to something this morning. She was out of her quilted housedress when I woke up at nine and sharply attired in a pair of polyester slacks with navy blue flats and dark beige hose. She's got on a pair of earrings she bought recently. Large cloisonné ducks. They swing as she moves her thin neck.

I stop reading the paper and listen. Mrs. Capp opens the freezer and it's difficult to hear what she's saying, but I can hear the cadence of her fluty voice.

"Sure," Satan says. "Okay." Ice clanks. Some chairs move. The back door opens. Shuts.

Satan as a Sunday-morning visitor. It seems appropriately absurd. A blatant metaphor for why I don't date. Why I pour over the *Times* (alone) on Sunday mornings, plan my weekends according to books on my shelf, homework, walks, and movies I haven't yet seen. The freedom of my newfound solitude still thrills me.

The initial phases were harder. When the graduate school acceptance letter came through my mail slot one Tuesday morning, Kevin was in my kitchen, slurping cereal. I grabbed it out of the heap of bills and advertisements, ripped it open with my thumb.

Kevin's face puckered when I showed it to him. "You're not going, are you?" I looked at his stubbly jaw, the one eyebrow that stood up like it had suffered some great shock.

"I don't know," I said.

Weeks later, during dinner at an overpriced Vietnamese restaurant, I broke the news. Women with bright teeth and dark, glistening hair sat with men in button-down shirts, leather bags stashed neatly beside their chairs. "I've accepted the offer," I told him.

His brown eyes, so familiar, so expressive, were utterly blank. I cringed. I knew I'd made a terrible mistake, and one for which I wouldn't be forgiven. The mistake was not in leaving California. It was telling him here, like this, the smell of steamed mussels between us like a fog.

"Everything all right?" our waitress asked.

"Oh, it's delicious," I said. I wanted her to stay, to sit down with us and tell us funny stories about herself. "But I'd like a beer."

"You too?" she said, turning to Kevin. He continued to stare at me for a beat. The world went still. Then his eyes teared and gaped; his hands flew to his throat.

The waitress smiled patiently.

"Kevin?" I said. He opened his mouth and his face turned a strange shade of red, then a deep shade of burgundy.

"He's choking!" I told the waitress.

The following minutes are somewhat blurry. I'd taken a CPR/General Emergency course but so long ago. When had I ever used it? And while he sat clutching his throat, I thought about how guilty I would feel if he died. The waitress pounded on Kevin's back and then one of the glossy-haired women at a nearby table ran over, wrenched the waitress's arm away, lifted Kevin to a vulnerable half-upright position, clasped her hands, and BAM, out flew the wad of noodles, onto the white tablecloth.

I dropped him off at his apartment and he got out of the car without kissing me. The relief I felt watching him go through the dirty glass doors has followed me out here. I'm still glad that Kevin is alive, those pink scars marking his thumbs, the noodles out of his airways. But I'm also glad not to be with him, walking through the glass doors, up the ammonia-scented stairway to his one-bedroom apartment.

Mrs. Capp and Satan are on the porch drinking lemonade. If I sit on my bed, in the corner of the room, I can see them through the window. And because the windows are so old, the seals broken, the glass rattling in strong wind, I can hear most of what they're saying.

"It's terrible to lose someone," I hear Satan say.

"It is," Mrs. Capp says sadly. "It's like the world is whisked away from you. Nothing looks the same."

Satan grunts. Mrs. Capp must recognize the irony of explaining loss to Satan, but it doesn't show on her face.

"I brought you a present," Satan says, gesturing to a small pink package. She gazes at it as if it were the correct ending to her sad thoughts. She's holding the package on her lap and I'm annoyed that I can't see what's inside when she carefully edges off the foil.

What gift does Satan bring on a Sunday morning? Apple chips? Tarot cards? Snakeskin barrettes?

"So sweet," she croons. She gets up, sits in his lap, and gives him a long, passionate kiss. She pulls away and Satan looks at her in the same way he looked at the headline on the paper. She rakes her pearly nails down the edge of his jaw, stands, gathers the empty glasses. I hear the back door open.

I jump off my bed, smooth out the wrinkles in my quilt. She pokes her head in.

"He's cute, isn't he?"

"Sure." The chirpiness of my voice is a giveaway that I've been spying, but she's too preoccupied to notice.

"Oh, gosh, Liza. Come outside and talk to him. I've got a really strong feeling about this one." When Mrs. Capp talks about men, she sounds as if she's dangling from a fine thread. She seems frightened of falling. Maybe this is why she lines them up one after the other: the next one can catch her if the thread snaps.

She goes out into the kitchen to refill their glasses. I yank off my pajamas and slide into the jeans and sweater I left by my bed the night before. Outside, the backyard brims with life. The brown grass is turning green again. The large oak tree has its first leaves. Satan smiles at me. I pull up a chair.

"How's it going?" I ask. I can tell from the lack of sheen on his eyes that he doesn't really want me to be there.

"Good," he says, wiping the edge of his lip. His limbs are excessively long in comparison to his compact torso. And he's not particularly good-looking. There's a lack of symmetry to his face. His eyes are crooked and small, and his mouth and nose are squishy. All of this under a giant forehead, his hairline receding.

Mrs. Capp flings herself through the door, her face a cramped expression of joy. She's brought me a lemonade as well.

"Satan's a housepainter," Mrs. Capp says to me as she settles onto her chair. He nods.

"I was just telling him that our house could use a little painting." This is true. The peach paint is peeling in the front and half the window frames are a glossy maroon while the other half are dirty white.

"Sure," he says, his voice gravelly. "We could probably

work out a trade." He directs this statement to Mrs. Capp and his head lowers slightly. His lids drop over those small blue eyes. Mrs. Capp shoots him a reprimanding glance, but lightens it with a purse of her lips, which, I notice, have a fresh coat of orangey lipstick.

Satan leans back in his chair and parts his legs. His hands dangle between his thighs. I catch a whiff of his smell. It's musky, rank, and a little dizzying—the kind of body odor you can't help breathing in repeatedly, though it seems inappropriate to do so.

There's a rising tide of energy at the table and it's making me uncomfortable. It seems that at any moment, Satan might lunge over the patio table with no regard to the tall glasses of lemonade, grasp Mrs. Capp with his clearly capable hands, and mash those soft features into her powdered neckline.

"So, how'd you get your name?" I ask. A chill comes over the porch. Satan doesn't take his eyes off Mrs. Capp. He's got the fingers of both hands pressed together and he's doing little push-ups with them. No one has anything to say.

I have never had any illusions about knowing the workings of Mrs. Capp's soul, but right now I feel particularly alienated. I knew she was a bit desperate, but there's an edginess to her need I didn't see before. Her neck looks more than thin, it seems breakable.

"We were thinking of going to a matinee," Mrs. Capp says. She wrinkles her eyes and nose.

I take the last cookie from the fancy platter on the table. Beside the platter is the CD Satan brought for Mrs. Capp in that pink foil. It's called *Music for the Living: Experiments in Joyful Sound.* That's just too much. Who is he trying to fool?

There's a shifting under the table. Satan's foot, clad in a dirty Converse high-top, creeps up Mrs. Capp's leg and his knee, in the process, bumps against my thigh. I set the CD down with a thwack. Mrs. Capp raises her eyebrows.

"Well," she says, "if we're going to go, I should put on a warmer sweater. I always get cold in theaters." She takes the CD and places it on the empty platter. Satan gathers the glasses and follows her into the house. I stay outside, looking at the oak tree trembling in the imperceptible wind.

After a few minutes, I get up and walk around the house. A large Dodge van is parked out front. Satan's van. The windows are tinted and a large, expandable ladder is secured to the top. There's a big dent in the rear bumper. I circle the van and I'm surprised to find a mural painted on the door of the driver's side. It's a crudely painted picture of the planet Earth. The continents make a green-brown yin-yang with the bright blue ocean. Underneath it is a red heart with the words ONE LOVE printed inside. The rest of the van is a sinister gray with a black stripe running along the base. I stand on my tiptoes and peer into the back. As I suspected, among some paint cans and roller brushes, a flannel sleeping bag covers a foam mattress. A tapestry is fastened to the ceiling.

Who is this man? Where did he come from? How long is he going to stay? Should I be concerned about my stuff?

For the first time since I moved here, I feel distinctly alone. Not solitary, but unseen. I don't miss anyone, exactly. Who would I miss? If Kevin were here he would claim to know things he didn't know. He would say that none of this was our business. He would shrug and suggest that we play ultimate Frisbee in the dog park.

The street is quiet. I can hear the movement of blood

through my body. I look at the peeling peach house in front
of me and kick the tire of the van. Nothing happens.

I go back inside. The door to Mrs. Capp's room is shut.
I stand in front of it, staring at the white paint. I wonder if
they've managed to leave without letting me know. This
seems unlikely. Mrs. Capp doesn't have a car and the bus
stop is right across the street. Then I hear a giggle. Several
giggles, a moan.

I know I should leave. I'm crossing a line by standing
here in front of her door. I should go back into my bedroom, read a magazine. Then there is a creaking sound.
Some talking. I get even closer.

"Oh, that's so strange," she says. Her voice sounds
husky, playful. "Stop it!" There's a cracking sound, like a
horsewhip. A squeal.

"Like this," he says. And then the words are muffled.

"Oh God!" she cries. The sound of rustling. Soon a
rhythmic thudding begins. I back away and walk aimlessly
into the kitchen.

Eavesdropping has only intensified the bad feeling. I
can't think of a single thing to do. Satan's denim jacket is
draped on a chair. A pack of cigarettes pokes from the top
pocket. I take one with the matchbook and go out onto the
porch. Mrs. Capp would throw a fit if she saw me smok-
ing, but it seems safe to assume she's preoccupied. I inspect
the matchbook, hoping it's from an incriminating place—
a strip joint or casino. But the matchbook just advertises a
brand of cigarettes. The foxglove that Mrs. Capp planted
shoots up from the raised beds and a few purple buds have
opened to the sun. I will a silence to take over my thoughts,
but before I'm even finished with the cigarette, a voice
comes from behind me.

"She's a fine woman, that Sondra." My heart skips, then a hot surge of blood races to my ears. He's standing in the doorway. I turn to see him adjust his privates through the canvas of his pants. He's so efficient. A real time manager. If he worked a service job, his face would be lacquered to a celebratory plaque.

It takes me a moment to register what he's just said. Fine woman. Who says "fine woman"? What could that possibly mean? Is it a euphemism for a good, easy lay? And he called her Sondra. I don't think I've ever heard anyone call her Sondra. Not even her mail comes addressed like that.

"Really a first-class broad," he says. He must be trying to get my goat. He lights a cigarette and leans lazily against the door frame, crossing his gangly legs. Mrs. Capp comes out in a coral wrap that matches her lipstick.

"Liza dear, do you think you can help me find my keys?" This must be a cue: she wants to conspire with me to get rid of Satan. She realizes she's slipped and now she wants a trusty female hand out of the mess. I stamp out the cigarette and breathe deeply. Mrs. Capp turns and I see Satan run a hand up the back of her leg and goose her. She giggles and swats his hand. He grins.

Inside the living room, Mrs. Capp begins to root around between the sofa cushions.

"Could you check around, dear?" she says. "Maybe they're underneath a magazine or something." I halfheartedly pick up the paper. Nothing. Carefully, I fold it along its creases and set it on top of the unread sections on the coffee table. Mrs. Capp scurries about, lifting picture frames off the mantel, patting pillows, straightening up as she looks.

"Maybe you left them in a pocket," I suggest.

"Well, it seems unlikely," she says. "But let's check." I follow her into her bedroom and almost keel over, the smell of sex is so strong. Her powder blue curtains are drawn and the bedsheets are tangled. Her fluffy comforter is pushed to one side and a condom wrapper lies torn and empty by the foot of the bed. With a swift movement she scoops up the comforter and settles it back on the mattress. I walk stiffly to her dresser and peer at the contents. There are the cloisonné ducks. This comforts me. She does seem the sort to take her jewelry off before a roll in the hay. I touch the earrings. They're cold and hard. I press the little hooks into my thumb. Her etched night sky box sits next to a glass paperweight with a miniature seal caught inside. On a slightly brown crocheted doily stands a framed photograph of Mrs. Capp's deceased parents. They look normal enough—her father dressed in military uniform, a mustache curling over his lip, her mother erect by his side, unsmiling.

"Where on earth could they be?" she says. Then she sees the condom wrapper and picks it off the ground, sticks it in her pocket. She meets my eyes and blushes slightly. I feel emboldened.

"Satan said you were a first-class broad," I tell her.

"Well isn't that sweet," she says. I study her face. Surely it's going to fall into something other than that dreamy smile.

"I told you, Liza, he's special. I can sense it."

I jam the hook into my thumb a little harder.

While Mrs. Capp goes through her jacket pockets, I try to imagine what my life would have been like had I followed Kevin up those stairs, into that dim apartment. He would have sulked for a while about his potential death while the sky outside darkened to black. I would have sat on the scratchy wool sofa, paging through a copy of some weathered novel Kevin kept on his bookshelf for show. He would have taken a shower, emerged wet and sullen, his brown hair sticking up in shiny cowlicks all over his scalp. Soon he would have nestled next to me, buried his face in my neck, forgiven me my lack of heroism, thanked God for sparing his life. We could have gone on like that, the scratchy sofa bothering our legs, into the great infinity. Would that really have been so bad?

"Here they are!" Mrs. Capp says. If the keys had hair, she'd give it a good-natured tousle. "They must have fallen off the night table." She clanks them in her palm. Little castanets.

I sit down on the bed and smile. "Don't do anything I wouldn't do," I tell her.

She winks at me. "Oh, Liza," she says. "You wouldn't do anything."

NO SMALL FEAT

F I WRITE THAT MY MOTHER DIED OF CANCER, NO ONE will publish this story—cancer being too ubiquitous. So, for this story, let's call it consumption. It's a romantic idea, anyway—the air hunger, the weakness.

My boyfriend Kierny is a writer, too. He claims to be a novelist, though apparently he also wrote a few stories while I was back in Idaho, adjusting my mom's meds, switching her oxygen tubes around. I found out about Kierny's story writing by accident. It was Saturday and I was in a bad patch, working and reworking the same fragments. A goose flying out of a woman's mouth. A child hit by a bus. Nothing was going anywhere.

"Why didn't you *tell* me?" Olivia demanded. I'd picked up the phone on the first ring, assuming it would be Kierny.

"What? What didn't I tell you?" Liv was a friend from graduate school. Everything excited her. Her own ears seemed to make her shrill with joy, but in spite of myself I felt a surge of hope.

"God, it's like the best one in the anthology, Sarah. You must be so proud."

I had four stories published the year before my mom died—a few in really good places. I'd been on a roll. The magazines came to me in shrink-wrap, my name shining out in glossy black or blue or pink. Did an editor somewhere forget to tell me she'd submitted one for a prize?

"It's an incredible rendering of your mother. Just amazing. There's even the way she did that thing when she ate—that thing with her teeth. Just a sec, you must know the scene. Here it is, page 239—"

"Liv, what are you talking about?" I asked.

"What do you *mean*?" she said. "Kierny's story in *Best American* . . . 'Consumed.'" I looked at the apple slices turning brown on my plate. "Sarah?"

"I didn't know about it," I said.

"Oh," Liv said. "Oops."

Kierny didn't pick up his phone, which was just as well; I couldn't formulate a thought. I drove to the bookstore.

It was probably a mix-up. Another Kierny. Another mother. Kierny had a competitive streak. Every time I had a story accepted he locked himself away for weeks, working to catch up. But we were honest. We'd been through hell together. The midnight phone calls after I wrestled my mother into bed—my anger the only thing available to me. He sat on the sofa those awful winter evenings, listening to me berate everyone—from the doctors to my closest friends—and he didn't try to reason with me. When she finally died, he drove all night from California to make the funeral, showed up in a wrinkled gray shirt and borrowed slacks. He greeted extended family. He cried when I cried. He shoveled dirt into her grave.

I could see the dust floating in the air of the bookstore. Huge skylights cut through the roof and the glossy paperbacks shone. There it was—on the wooden display table with the latest by Eggers, Chabon. *Best American*—its bright orange cover beckoning. I opened it. A few big names and then: Kierny McAllister . . . "Consumed."

Why hadn't he told me about this? I flipped to his bio. Kierny McAllister is a North Carolina native living in Berkeley, California. "Consumed" is his first published story.

The fucker, I said aloud. A woman with a toddler in tow shot me a look. I shot one back.

The fucker.

I brought the book to the cashier and slapped it on the counter. I couldn't even read the first line. With the book in the trunk, I went to find Kierny. He was probably at his studio writing more stories about my life, more stories about my dead mother. For God's sake, Kierny, I thought, get your own death. Get your own pain.

Kierny's studio belonged to the McDonald's of art studios. A company bought up vacant lots around California and erected these cheaply constructed corrugated-metal buildings. Kierny had a spot on the ground floor next to a woman who made custom tarot cards and animal-shaped soap. Outside his open door sat a bench and a bunch of happy-looking poppies.

He'd left his door ajar.

"So were you ever going to tell me?" I said.

Some kind of grease had worked its way across his glasses. Papers were scattered around him on the floor. He looked annoyed.

"Hi, Sarah," he said.

I went to hold up the book, but I didn't have it, so I ran back to the car, unlocked the trunk, and ran back. I held it like a little orange picket sign.

"Look what I found! Someone named Kierny McAllister is writing stories about my mom!"

"Sarah, Jesus." Kierny turned back to his lit-up screen and saved his document. Then he calmly closed his laptop. It made a soft click.

"So you read it?" he asked.

My arm skin prickled. "No, not exactly, not yet."

"You haven't read it and you're this mad?" He raised his thick eyebrows.

"I can't believe you'd write a story about my mom dying, send it out, get it published—and never run it by me."

He pushed his hair off his forehead. "I was afraid you'd have a bad reaction," he said. "And you are." Kierny took a breath and held it, gazed down at the poppies. I moved my foot back to squish one.

"It's about death, Sarah, and I didn't want to bring up more death stuff for you."

"You didn't want to bring up more death stuff for me? Are you kidding? This is *my mom* you wrote about. For you this was a story, but for me it was *real*."

"Shhh. Sarah, there are people working here."

I'd always thought Kierny was adorable—his blackish hair and crooked nose. His way of leaning when he walked, as if it would make him less tall.

Now Kierny looked a little anemic. I could see his

wormy temple veins. And he had a cold. He looked plugged up.

I turned around, went back to my car, drove home.

With a tall glass of whiskey, I tried to settle myself long enough to read the story.

I couldn't do it. It was the middle of the day, too hard to read. I shut the blinds to approximate night. I turned on all the lights. I fed my cat. I washed the dishes. I felt dirty. I felt like crying. I turned on the shower and stood under it.

All the stories I had written about my mom's death had come back with little slips of paper. *We just get so many stories about cancer* (oops, I mean consumption), *it's impossible to publish another! We do admire your writing, though, so keep sending us work!* Or *The grief is palpable—you've allowed us to see it in a whole new way. No small feat! But we're afraid grief isn't enough for us. We need a larger worldview. Maybe submit to our next theme issue: CLASH: Ugandan Politics and the New Urban Male. . . .* One editor suggested I wait until I was in the next phase of my life before sending another story. It got so obnoxious that I stopped sending the stories out. No one wants to hear about mortality, I figured. Dead moms, dead dads—they're a dime a dozen.

I took a Xanax.

I opened the book.

I kept imagining what it would feel like to get closer to her—to hold her, undress her, run my hands over the strange rubber of her skin. Even if she was my girlfriend's mother— my girlfriend's dying mother, in that state—so near to death— she was magnetic.

*　　*　　*

Okay, fine. She didn't die of consumption, she died of cancer. And like most cancer deaths, it wasn't pretty. Her breast turned purple, then black, then it ate itself. Her skin grew tough and red. Sores opened on her lips and forehead. The tumor grew so big it was like a globe pressing out of her chest. She smelled like fish and sweat and unflushed pee. She was delirious for weeks, coming in and out of this world.

My mother was trained in classical ballet. She stood erect and held her head high. Before she got sick, she used to coil her thick hair in a bun at the nape of her neck. Men smiled at her in grocery stores. Students filled every dance class she offered.

She was sick for eleven years. The treatments and steroids made her hair change texture. It fell out and came back wiry, streaked with a dark, flat gray. Then it fell out again and came back in patches. Her skin took on a chemical glow. She gained weight. She wasn't magnetic in her death state. Kierny could barely stand to be in the same room with her. When she was in the final stages, moaning, balling her fists, rolling back her eyes—he wouldn't even visit. He stayed in California, apparently imagining all this, working extra hours at his magazine job.

I was alone when she died. As her body morphed, swelled, and rotted, I held her hands. I wiped the oozing. I don't have any siblings. And my father, he's not around.

I'm straying. I'm writing about death again. Damn it. It's become a habit. Is the key to insert sex?

Gratuitous Sex Scene #1

The night after my mom died, Kierny arrived in Boise. I don't remember very much about that evening. There was whiskey and beer and lots of casserole. Some of my mom's friends had arrived and were answering the phone. Dinnertime passed, then it was night. We went upstairs to my childhood bedroom.

He held me and I tried to relax. My body wouldn't settle. I felt violent. I wanted to throw the little porcelain box off my bureau and watch it shatter, hurl books through the window, leave bloody scratches up my own arms. And so I pulled away from him, pushed him down on the bed, undid the button of his jeans.

It wasn't sex I wanted, not really. I wanted to watch him under a spell. I wanted to control him.

"Are you sure?" he asked. I untied his shoes, pulled off his boxers, looked at his pink penis, lying a little lopsided across his stomach. I took it in my hands, then in my mouth. It pulsed and quivered. Finally he started panting. I went faster, pulled at the base—and then he came all over my quilt.

"Oh wow," he said.

"Yeah," I said.

But I still felt violent.

Kierny, you might be interested to know, has both of his parents. He's from Chapel Hill. His dad is a physicist. His mom is a pediatrician. He has a sister named Wendy who is happily married to a veterinarian. His younger brother Anton is at Yale.

Kierny is a well-adjusted person. In fact, Grover Edgar, a student in our graduate workshop, once said you could tell from Kierny's prose that he hadn't felt a whole lot of pain in his life. "It's like what an alien might imagine human pain would feel like," he said. At the time I'd thought Grover was kind of an asshole. His dad killed himself when Grover was young and it was all he could write about.

"Red Rover, Red Rover, help Grover get over it," Kierny joked.

. . . in that state—so near to death—she was magnetic.

You want more of Kierny's story? Well, go buy it. It's under copyright. I'm only providing a synopsis.

The story takes some funny turns, Kierny being a funny guy. He's with Terri (the fictional me) and Lucinda (my fictional mom) while Lucinda is dying. Terri is having a lot of trouble managing the daily tasks—administering meds and doing laundry—because Terri is obsessed with yoga and detox diets. (I am most certainly *not* obsessed with yoga or detox diets.) Terri watches yoga videos on the television in the basement, leaving the male character, Theo, with plenty of time for monkey business.

Of course, Lucinda and Theo never actually have an affair. But they do have numerous meaningful conversations on the nature of life and death. Pithy ones, even. But a particularly stunning scene involves Lucinda fantasizing about having a one-night stand.

"I was too well behaved in my life," she says to him. "I wish I'd broken a few more rules." In this scene, she's just been bathed by a nurse. She reclines in the bed, her hair wrapped in a turban. (Hair? A turban?) She won't tell him the details of her wishes, but in her eyes he sees a film strip: a dark house, white linens, soft light, and the deep line down a woman's spine.

He feels a powerful pull and says, "I think I need to get a beer." Lucinda rubs her dry feet together suggestively.

At the bar, which he goes to alone in Terri's truck, he meets a young undergrad, Fiora. Fiora's a biology major. She's got dark skin, long dark hair, and a small diamond in her nostril. She's nothing like poor Terri (who's milk and honey pretty, but who's turned a little stringy and dour during these hard months). Fiora's eyes are coy, her lashes shine. She laughs at Theo's jokes and her fingers travel up the inseam of his pants.

Outside, on the gravel of the parking lot, he bites at her jaw. *She smelled like oatmeal and coal,* Kierny wrote.

(Kierny once told me about a girlfriend he'd had at summer camp when he was fifteen. She smelled like oatmeal, he'd said. And when I said that was kind of a dumpy thing to smell like, he disagreed vehemently, saying oatmeal was about as earthy as you could get.)

What do you think happens? Yes! They sleep together! At her dorm. Beneath a large tapestry with camels on it.

Terri doesn't find out, and, strangely, Theo doesn't feel guilty. He feels more in love with Terri and more alive than he's ever felt. Tenderness overwhelms him, and so, a week later, he tries it again. Only this time, it's much more dangerous—it's with Diego, the nurse.

(Now, caretakers are not a sexy lot. In Idaho, we got a lot of women with dyed red hair and smoker's coughs chattering endlessly about cats and car payments. Some of them were expert crocheters, crossword puzzlers, or cardsharps, but none of them—not one—exuded sexual magnetism.)

Diego is a svelte biracial man, paying his way through a graduate degree in English by working nights caring for hospice patients. He's got—these are not my words—"skin the color of burned butter" and "eyes one shade paler than teal." Theo is not gay—he had one "experimental" experience in college during a spin the bottle game when he was trying to impress a bisexual coed. But Diego is flaming gay—and unmistakably sexual. He has a gay man's flair for fashion. Even while making house calls to dump commodes and wipe sores, he's wearing tight T-shirts and form-fitting pants.

At one point Theo almost tells Lucinda what he's done, he wants her to see him in a new light: a man with free will, able to live out her fantasies. He wants them to have a virtual affair. But before he says anything she takes his hands and he feels an opening in his body, as if she already knows, blah blah blah.

Eventually, Lucinda dies (she just closes her weary eyes and kaput! she fades). Theo realizes that she is gone, but her spirit is everywhere, lives inside of them all, and this gives him a kind of peace and a renewed zest for love and life.

It's an annoying story, isn't it?

So palpable! So felt! I imagine the editors said. *You've helped us to see death in a new way! No small feat!*

I don't get it. I truly don't. Which is why I'm going to write this story, call it fiction, and then apply to law school.

I didn't sleep the night I read that story. Instead, I sat up with a photograph of my mother, taken three weeks before she died. In it, the two of us are sitting on the brown overstuffed sofa. My arm is around her shoulders. Her face is gray and the oxygen tubes drape over her chest. One of her eyes is drifting. My face is close to her ear, like I am whispering something to her.

Don't die, I'm saying—you can see it in the way I'm clutching her nightgown with my hand.

Gratuitous Sex Scene #2
(Or, "A Brief Story of My Conception, August 1977")

It's New York—Soho. And this is the night my mother will meet my father. My mother, Brenda Oberlin, has just turned twenty-three. She's long and thin and wears tight jeans and flowing tunics.

She doesn't know it yet—that this night will be fateful. She knows this: she is not a lesbian, as much as she likes Alice, as pretty as Alice is with that sly face, shiny lips, and shocking black hair. She's been sleeping with Alice for three weeks, trying to feel the energy. They've come to this art opening because Alice is a painter. She's friends with a friend of the artist. It's a large room and it smells like dust with something sweet mixed in—nail polish or turning meat.

The artist is a skinny man with a grin that makes him look like he's got food in his mouth. He's less handsome than Brenda's usual boyfriends—less handsome but more talented. She likes the strange birds he paints, their beaks menacing but their eyes patient and all-knowing. He's wearing a strand of purple beads over a linen shirt. He's drinking beer with a straw.

She stands near Alice in the corner, eyeing him as he greets guests. And then, when he backs out of the room for a cigarette, she follows.

She says, "I just love your work," and then feels stupid. She's young and it's summer. Her body is light and airy, no different from the heat off the building, the eggy air coming out of the vent they stand over, the white East Coast sky.

She bums a cigarette and imagines that his hand doesn't stop at hers, but reaches past her, grabs her behind her ribs, pulls her in. She feels his body—so much more substantial than Alice's—his dick hard against her thigh, and the heat of the sky and warmth of her own blood conspire to make her look too deeply at him, woozily almost, as if they have already crawled in and out of bed a hundred times.

They talk about the neighborhood, a Russian diner. They leave together, despite the guests inside, the paintings lit by expensive lights that shine down from the windows to the dark pavement. They buy a bag of M&Ms and a fifth of whiskey and start kissing in front of his building.

Keys, a heavy door, a room with exposed brick and a ratty sofa. His hands are large and they slide around her, hoist her up against the wall.

"You smell good," he says. She's wearing Alice's Chanel—but under that she smells like an athlete.

He carries her over to his sofa—the bed's lofted, too hard to get to—and he slides off her moccasins, her jeans. She's drunk. He's drunk. It's quick and sloppy but it feels good, slippery and exciting, no talking, no negotiating. They slide off the sofa onto his shag rug. "I'm leaving next week," he tells her before he drifts off. He's got a hand in her hair. "A fellowship. I'll be gone a long time." She shrugs. He sticks his fingers inside her to feel his wetness there. Again she is heat and headiness and the feel of her skin on a soft shag rug.

For two days after I read the story, I didn't hear from Kierny. It seemed to me that he was too much of a coward to call, but that's not his version. His version is that he was giving me time to recover. When he finally did call, his voice sounded locked up.

"How're you doing?" he said. Was it guilt making him sound that way? Because in his tone I heard deep annoyance, as if I'd read that story against his will.

"I'm all right," I said.

"I had to process it," Kierny said. "What you were going through was hard on me, too. You know it's fiction, it's a fantasy—and I didn't tell you because, well, I just kept putting it off. I didn't want to hurt you. I'm sorry."

I looked at the crack in my ceiling.

I don't have a patent on death. I wouldn't want one. Really, he can have the subject—the whole big feat of it. I'd love to write stories about surfing teenagers, international spies, funny grandmothers, dogs that fly. But death is my map, the thing I've been living next to for years.

"Look, it would be easier to talk this over in person," Kierny said.

He arrived with a bag of groceries. A bottle of wine.

He looked sheepish in the doorway, and for a moment I could see outside of my anger. One time Kierny and I hiked to a lake in the Sierras, both of us singing Beatles and Springsteen until our voices cracked, still singing while we swam naked in the lake. Then some teenagers came out of the woods and pelted us with pistachios. Another time I crashed his car into a pole in the parking garage and he flipped out and looked like a moose and I told him and he yelled at me and then we both started laughing and Kierny spilled his Coke.

The baguette stuck out of the bag and he looked confused, like he wasn't sure whether to challenge or console me.

"I brought salami," he said.

*   *   *

She says, "You're on your own now, kiddo."

"I know," I say.

"I'm gone."

"I know."

"You don't believe it."

"No, how can I? You were just here."

"I'm not speaking to you. You're imagining this."

"Why am I failing at everything, Mom? Why is it all falling away?"

She's not in the sky, in my body. She's not in her bones in the pine box in the grave. She is simply gone. My father—I used to try to look for him by attempting to track down old paintings, but he never became big—someone else probably painted his birds more successfully. I imagined them, the two of them, the feelings they once had—feelings that must have seemed consuming: they were hungry or tired or angry or ashamed. I imagined that night between them, the heat on their skin, the dizziness, the longing. And I reached for Kierny then, as he was eating a piece of salami. I pulled him in close, my hands behind his ribs.

I could dump him the next day and write this story. There was time for that. But now there was pressure on my cheeks and nose, like the beginning of drunkenness or grief.

"Are you sure?" Kierny asked, leaning in, his damp hands traveling up my back. His breath was meaty, spicy.

I unbuttoned my shirt and let it fall away as I climbed on top of the table.

"I'm sure," I said.

WEIGHT

When I was thirteen, the mother I knew from childhood began to bury herself in a very different body. A beard of runny flesh grew below her chin and her thighs chafed as she walked. The clothes she wore, once tailored to show off her narrow waist and long legs, turned to large T-shirts, elastic waist jeans. Only her nose remained, fine and sharp, like a knife cutting out from dough. Four years later, my father left. I stood in the dark hallway after she told me and watched her cry silently into a washcloth. *It's your fault,* I thought. *You drove him away.*

When I went to college, I hung a photograph of her young and lean on my dorm room mirror. "Your mom's pretty," people remarked when they visited. "She looks like you." The photograph was taken at my mother's sweet-sixteen party in Sheepshead Bay, Brooklyn, in 1965. She poses in a powder blue sequined dress, her bangs curled over her face, the rest of her hair piled above it in a hive of clashing swirls. She stands jaunty and sure, hand on the hip, one foot thrust slightly out. Her smile both radiates and challenges.

If she'd married Joel Greenbaum—the short one with adoring eyes and a monobrow, who came to the party bearing the heart pendant I still wear (the one with the diamond so small, it looks like the gleam in a beetle's eye)—I imagine her life would have taken a dramatically different turn. She would not have married my father, a stockbroker who left her sitting alone in a big house in California while he dealt with big accounts overseas. She would not have buried her howling loneliness beneath a buffer of flesh.

It's true that she wouldn't have had me (or not exactly me, though who knows how souls get doled out). She might have other children, though—a son who organized unions in Manhattan, a daughter with good taste in furniture and the fertility of a rabbit. But Joel married my mother's friend Mara instead. She's the plain one next to my mother, in what looks like a handmade frock.

Just after my thirty-first birthday, I put on a brown skirt, the one I wear when I know I'll have a particularly rough day at work. It has feminine ruffles and calms even the most beastly attorney. It didn't fit. The zipper strained nearly at its base and a thick mass of belly squished over the embroidered waist. I fought with that zipper for a good ten minutes. By the time my husband, Ed, came out of the bathroom, I was sweating the rank sweat of the distressed.

"So you gained a few pounds," Ed said, grabbing his trousers from the hanger. "You still look great. Get a new skirt."

"I don't want a new skirt! I want *this* skirt!" And I tugged the zipper so hard I ripped it right out of the fabric. Ed snickered and went to kiss me, but I dodged him, horrified. My pants still fit, but they hung badly, and the impenetrable calm that made me the best mediator in the office vaporized. Over the big oak table that morning, a fight broke out. The complainant threw a water glass against a painting.

My best friend, Kara, listened to me cry that night on the phone. "Lori," she said. "You don't get to have your twenty-year-old body for the rest of your life. Your metabolism slows. It happens to the best of us. I gained fifteen pounds when Cory was born."

"But my mom was fat," I said. "I can't be fat."

"You're not fat," she said. "You're not even close to fat. You were skinny and now you're thin."

When she first got sick, I drove my mother to the doctor's. "If you really want to know what I think," the doctor said. He was small with an elfin face and silver glasses. "I think you should lose some weight." My mother looked past him. "Cancer travels in lipids," he said.

We went out to dinner that night. Hoping to be a good influence, I ordered a spinach salad. She ordered the prime rib. "Cancer travels in lipids," I said to her.

"Leave me alone," she said. Every time she took a bite of that steak, I grew more and more furious. She chose that steak over my father, over another year of life. She chose that steak over me.

The night she died, I called the mortuary and two greasy young men in black suits came with a gurney. The darkness outside swirled into pink dawn. I filled out forms and answered questions. They lifted her body off the bed and headed toward the front door, but when they tilted her down the steps, one of them buckled under her weight and almost dropped her. I saw it: my mother slowly wedging against the wall, the three of us squatting, trying to roll her over. "Sorry," the man said. I could see a trace of laughter flit across the men's faces, but they quickly sobered, heaved, and off she went.

The night of the skirt incident, Ed slept peacefully beside me. His hairline receded slightly and the shine of his large forehead gave me a moment's reprieve. Then I felt all the facts in my life boil down to one: I needed to lose this weight. Not within a season, not within a month. I needed to lose it as quickly as it appeared: overnight. And if I didn't, the future was a dark black cavern and it had no words.

I found my slippers and went into the study. It took me two hours of reading and scrolling, typing various phrases into the search engine and registering in chat rooms to find it: the diet known only to a few gray-faced girls; a diet that, if followed correctly, the girls claimed, not only made you quickly thin, but made you *stay* thin. It was a little odd. But every testimonial sang its praises.

I lost ten pounds in a week and NOT just water weight! OMG what a lifesaver!

My boyfriend says I look sexy as hell!

My size 00 is baggy :)

On and on the girls went, posting pictures of their midriffs, measurements of their arms and thighs.

Their method was unorthodox, sure. But I could do it for the short term, get back into my skirt. Then I'd stop the diet and start running again.

I told Ed about it in the morning.

"You've lost your mind," he said.

I tried to explain that I just needed his help for now, that I felt urgency because of my mother's early death. That to be fat was the worst fate imaginable, worse even than cancer because at least cancer earned you pity. Ed cut a banana into a bowl of cereal and turned to face me.

"Listen to yourself," he said. "You want me to lock you in a dark room and cause you some deep, twisted humiliation because a website says it'll make you thin? I'm Ed, by the way. Nice to meet you." He didn't kiss me when he left that morning and I got dressed alone in my closet, imagining my old stomach, flat as a book.

The rules of the diet were as follows: you ate very little for breakfast, then before lunch someone you loved locked you in a dark space, like a closet, and berated you. This ruined your appetite. The girls complained of sleeplessness and wild emotional ranges, but in terms of its effectiveness, the diet had no rival.

If Ed wouldn't do it (I had not expected him to; he counsels teenagers for a living), then I had to resort to someone else.

A little over a year ago my father came to my apartment with a gift certificate to an outdoor store and told me that he knew it had been wrong to leave like that, that he did not expect me to forgive him, but hoped that I would allow him to be part of my life.

I held the gift certificate as I listened. He'd clearly prepared this speech, and when it concluded, he had nothing more to say. And in the complicated way of abandoned children everywhere, I tried to find ways of excusing him. He didn't get what he needed from his own parents. His mother cried daily, kneading a handkerchief with red fingers. His father's arms jerked from drinking. And my mother—I imagined him trying to make love to her, trying to find that jaunty, sequined girl who intoxicated him with her particular blend of slyness and naïveté. But she was lost inside that thick case of skin. Generosity lasted only so long, though, and inevitably my forgiveness turned to rage.

I never spent the gift certificate. I taped it to the refrigerator with bills that needed to be paid and a photograph of Kara's two-year-old, his face smeared with peas. I told my father he could call me from time to time, but I let the machine pick up his messages and rarely returned his calls.

He owed me one.

I called him from work, before my first mediation. He sounded relieved, as if a heavy parcel he'd been negotiating had momentarily vanished.

"I was wondering if you could help me with something," I said.

"Of course! What do you need? Money?"

And from there, I explained the skirt situation and the diet. I reminded him of Mom's problems, her untimely death, how obesity had complicated her treatments—

"I know," he snapped.

"It's just temporary," I said. "If it's as effective as people say it is, I'll have all this weight off in less than two weeks. Ed won't do it, so I'm asking you."

"You want me to berate you?"

I straightened some files on my desk, cleaned lint from my keyboard. The light for the other line lit up.

"How much weight is it?" he asked.

"Maybe five pounds," I said.

"Can't you just go jogging? Cut out dessert for a few weeks? That's not a lot of weight." The red light on the phone flashed, flashed, and finally ceased.

"It's not like I've asked you for much in the past," I said. From the silence, I thought maybe he'd hung up.

"Fine," he said curtly. "I can try."

All of the furniture in my father's condo had been purchased in the months following his third divorce. He'd hired an interior decorator with a preference for modern lines and the place looked like the waiting room in a posh European salon. For a while, we sat on his white leather sofa and he asked me polite questions about Ed and my job, blinking fast as he did so.

In his mid-sixties now, my father still looked dapper. He walked with a swagger and his hair grew glossy and thick. Even though he'd retired, he wore an Italian dress shirt with lines of color so thin they disappeared when he turned from side to side. He'd never had trouble attracting women. Kara, in high school, thought I didn't notice when she followed him around the kitchen, flipping her blond hair. She listened to him talk about how women in France took care of themselves and allowed him to refill her glass of fizzy lemon soda. "Your dad has a way of making women feel beautiful," she remarked in the darkness of my bedroom. But I knew this father appeared only for other women. He looked right past my mother and me.

After the awkward talking, we migrated to his spare bedroom, where the closet sat empty save for a folding chair. The sports coats, ski equipment, and scuba gear he stored there were stacked on the bed.

He scratched the back of his head as I shut myself in. A line of light came in around the door. My high heels burrowed into the plush carpet. I imagined what it felt like to be a baby, swaddled in blankets, shielded from the bright lights of the outside world.

"Okay!" I said. The hollow closet door did nothing to buffer sound and I could hear the bed roll on the wood floor as my father sat.

The young women on the website rarely elucidated the details of the berating. "Obviously, the sessions are private," one of the administrators wrote. "The most effective subjects are those closest to your heart." She suggested various topics, in case your loved one had difficulty finding ways to shame you. "It's always better to find your own path," she wrote. "But in rare cases, this proves too difficult and dieters get mired in a lack of creative topics. General insecurities can be unearthed: body size, body odor, body hair, quality of voice, etc. Specific instances of embarrassment or disappointment might be utilized (e.g., have you been made a fool in public?). Sexual issues often provide good fodder: abortions, infertility, and sexually transmitted disease."

Until then, I had not considered what my father might say. This tire of belly felt like an omen, the gateway to a familiar, unwanted future, and the goal of losing it shined so bright, it blinded me. I took it in my fists and squeezed until my fingers left small imprints of ache. Something close to my heart? Would he, this man absent for most of my adult life, have the information necessary to make good on this plan? Did he have an arsenal? A list of ways I disappointed him, the things I did that drove him away?

The feeling of being swaddled turned into a feeling of being bound. My father cleared his throat.

"You look so much like your mother when she was your age," he said. "It can be a little disconcerting." A motor behind the wall began to whir, making my chair vibrate slightly. I crossed my legs and my arms. I wanted it—the feeling of being shot from a cannon, hurtling out into open sky. I wanted the shock and blinding pain of whatever he would say if it would lead me toward a life of discipline and resolve.

"Dad?" I said. He didn't respond. When I cracked open the closet door, he looked ashen.

"I'm getting older, Lori," he said. He placed his hands on his knees and bowed toward them. I sat next to him on the bed.

A small tear dribbled and fell off his cheekbone, getting lost in his dark stubble. He wrung his hands.

"I don't think I can do this," he said.

Never once, in my memory of him, did he make my mother dinner or take her, spontaneously, to look at the robins nesting in a tree out back. My mother made dinner. My mother noticed the robins. I had asked him one thing, one simple thing in thirty-one years, and he could not provide even that.

"You can do it," I said. But he averted his eyes and studied the edge of the shag rug.

"I told your mother that she disgusted me, that she looked like a cow, that if she didn't stop stuffing her fat face I would leave her."

My scalp pulled tight.

"She went on diet after diet, drank those shakes, and went to groups, but the whole time I wanted to marry Jana. I came home from London that year, it was nineteen eighty-nine, and I'd been gone for more than two months. She'd lost thirty pounds. Do you remember that? She looked so happy. And do you know what I thought? I thought she was doing it to try to trap me. That she knew about Jana and was torturing me by losing that weight." He pressed his fingers into his jaw. "I told her I didn't think she looked any different—and that I was leaving her." My father's face cinched up. "This isn't what you came here for. You wanted me to tell you that you embarrass me, that I think you're ugly or dim, but Lori, I've already been down this road." He reached out and put his hands on my thighs. It shocked me to feel them there, their pawlike weight. "It doesn't work," he said. His hands slid off, back to his own lap. "I think you should like yourself, Lori—and try to be happier than your mother was."

I saw my mother, loaded on Valium and Fentanyl, two months before she died, walking unsteadily into the kitchen to get a handful of chips. But on the way back to the couch, the world swooped and she lost her balance, falling against the counter, bag of chips in hand. "Mom!" I yelled, rushing toward her. Corn chips scattered around us like dull confetti. With a kitchen rag, I stopped the bleeding from the side of her head. She would die, right there, in a pile of blood-soaked chips, I thought. And there was nothing I could do. She didn't die; she put her hand to her head and told me to stop making a fuss. But it was too late. I already felt it: what it meant to be left utterly and ter-rifyingly alone.

"You're right—this isn't what I came here for." I grabbed my father's hand and lifted up my shirt partway, enough to reveal the pad of flesh.

"Touch it," I said. He recoiled. I yanked on his arm and he loosened. I pressed his hand into my belly. His fingers felt cool and damp.

"Lori, stop," he said. I let him go. His hand looked shrunken on the bed. I waited to see if he'd lift it, but he didn't move at all.

I walked back to the closet, shaking.

"Do it," I said to him, slamming the door. The closet felt alive, buzzing with more than the motor behind the wall.

"You look like a fat cow," he said softly. "And if you don't stop stuffing your face, Ed will leave you."

We sat with those words between us for a while. I wanted them. They soothed me. When I opened the door, carefully, slowly, he looked up at me.

"What you must have been through," he said. "With her sickness, her death. I can't imagine."

"No, you can't," I said. "But this isn't about that. This is about my diet."

"Lori," he said. He looked both tired and afraid. "This is not about your diet." We stared at each other, the way a deer and coyote might stare at each other in a field. Then I left.

Ed listened as I ranted about it that night. His face looked closed, his teeth shut tight.

"Would you be able to do that to someone?" he finally asked.

"What? Abandon my daughter with her dying mother?"

"No. Would you be able to lock someone up and berate them?" I had not touched my salad. The lettuce looked damp and cold.

"What does that have to do with anything?"

"I don't know what you want from him."

"I want him to help me for once."

"You want to punish him," Ed said. I squashed a piece of avocado through the tines of my fork. He got up and took the salad away, cleared the dishes. I stared at the cupboards.

"I don't want to get fat," I said. "I don't want to become my mother."

"Then don't become her," Ed said. "And don't become your father either, while you're at it." He went outside to water the plants.

My mother took me to the mall when I returned from my second year of college. We stood in front of the makeup counters and read the names of lipsticks. I glanced up to ask her what she thought of a shade and caught her looking at herself in one of the mirrored walls. She had painted her lips a garish red that brought out the broken veins in her cheeks. She shook her head. "Your fat, ugly mother," she said, grabbing a Kleenex and wiping the red away. She smiled at me as if to erase the moment, but it wouldn't go; it's still right here, lodged in my memory.

"It wasn't her weight," my father said to me. He had shown up outside my apartment after dinner in a light raincoat and freshly pressed pants. A few drops of rain glittered on his hair and shoulders. Wet wind blew in from the covered breezeway. I hadn't noticed the rain as I argued with Ed, but now I saw it, the sky clogged and gray. "I left because I thought I could be happier with someone else. And it wasn't true." He stood framed in the doorway, the silver-black night behind him. "I loved your mother," he said.

The night she fell, I cleaned up the chips from the floor and blamed them for the loneliness, for my father's absence, for her failing body. I piled them on the counter and crushed them to bits with my fists before throwing them in the trash. I didn't speak to her the next morning. She had no memory of falling, though, and so my tactic was unsatisfying.

"Why are you mad at me?" she asked, drugs smearing her focus. She sat over a bowl of cereal and watched the frozen strawberries bob. I didn't answer.

"There's no time for this," she said. "We don't have time to argue."

And whose fault is that? I wanted to scream. We would have had time if you had not eaten that steak, if you had been stronger! If you hadn't given in to this!

It rained that day, too. Her gaze turned from the strawberries to the driveway, the pavement growing darker from the water.

"I hope someday you can forgive everyone," she said. "Including yourself."

My skin hid all the things going on beneath. But for a moment, I feared my father could see through me—that my body had the acetate pages in an anatomy book—a woman in a shirt and skirt lifts to become the vascular system, skeletal system—and then finally just a shell: her uterus, lungs, intestines.

"Can I come in?" he asked, brushing rain from his hair. A few cars sped past, their headlights flickering. I thought of slamming my palms on the thick of his chest, pressing him out into blackness. I thought of shutting the door on him—the way he would look, forlorn. But he didn't wait for me to do these things; he just walked in, my father, out of the rain.

CELIA'S FISH

THE GOLDFISH CELIA CHOOSES SEEMS TO LEAP INTO the little green net, then into the bag from the net. Gerard wonders if it has some sort of mental problem. The fish is fat, fatter than its counterparts, and there's something mean and angular about its face. All the other fish look blank.

"Here you go," the kid with the net says; he snaps the rubber band around the top of the bag and hands it to Celia. The kid has rubbery skin. When he talks, it sounds like his tongue's engorged. His *r*s don't come out. Celia is eight. She holds the bag tenderly and delivers it to the counter. Gerard follows his daughter, extracting some change from his pocket.

Mandy's Pet Oasis is in the back of a drugstore, located next to racks of cheap flip-flops and mirrored sunglasses. It's been here for years, though before today, Gerard had never been inside. Most of the lighting comes from the fish tanks along one wall, giving the whole store a gloomy, cinematic feel. Behind shelves of dog bowls, cat litter, and plastic fish castles, a few world-weary puppies stare through the wire of their pens. According to the laminated signs tacked above them, they're twenty percent off.

"You got a tank?" the kid asks. "'Cause we got it on special today. Tank, filter, pebbles, food, castle, treasure chest, and pH stuff. All together." Gerard notices that a little knob of silver glints from the kid's mouth. The kid gestures to a tank on a card table, filled with colorful plastic castles and reeds, wrapped in cellophane.

"We have a bowl," Gerard says. It's not true, exactly, but Marsha said she'd bring one over later. The fish is a dollar. It glares at Celia from the bag, but she's examining kitty collars on a wire tree next to the register.

"You got your fish?" Gerard asks her. She nods and drags the bag off the counter religiously, as though it's full of golden powder.

Gerard watches his daughter as she walks out of the store. She's been dressing herself lately. Today it's grape-colored shorts that have gotten too tight and a wrinkled pink shirt. She's a strange girl, pale and brooding. And lately she's taken to walking crookedly, touching her shoulder to a wall, bouncing off it, then finding the next available surface to touch. She's got her mother Ellie's hair—or at least what Ellie's hair used to be—white blond, fine. It hangs straight down her back, ending in wispy curls that dissolve into the air.

"Hang a left, Celia-bean," he says. A display of beach balls has distracted her. She doesn't look at him, touches her shoulder to the display, and then heads diagonally out of the small complex of stores, cradling the little bag in the crook of her elbow.

Gerard watches Celia navigate through the sparse

parking lot. She touches her shoulder to each car as she walks toward their blue Honda. Gerard unlocks the passenger door and Celia slides in with a grimace. The car is hot, airless, and it hurts Gerard's legs to sit on the black vinyl. He rolls down his window but there's no breeze. He glances at the fish on Celia's lap. It's still glaring, this time at his leg. And as he turns the key, he imagines that someone has planted a car bomb beneath them, the entire car will burst into flames, and they will explode with it, body parts flying, hair burning, fish turning into a demon bird and fluttering off into the sky.

It's a short drive up to the hills where they live, and Gerard doesn't feel like talking. Marsha'd mentioned once that it was easier to have difficult conversations in the car—you couldn't see the other person's face—and sometimes when he's driving Celia around he thinks he should say something to her. *I know how hard this must be for you. I don't know what to say to make this better. We're a team, you and me, and we'll get through it.* All the words sound stupid in his head and he can't bear to say things he doesn't mean. Maybe somewhere in that eight-year-old mind, she understands the whole situation better than he does.

Gerard pulls into the garage and Celia bolts out of the car.

"I'm showing Mommy the fish," she announces, and with her side crammed against the railing, she runs, leaning into the wall so that it looks like she's being lifted up the steps by a magnetic force. When Gerard follows, only minutes later, he finds Celia in his bedroom, stuck by the dresser. Ellie looks terrible; she's been crying and her face is blotchy through the sweat and grayish sheen. Her eyes are too wide. Vomit is cooling in the pan they keep near the bed.

"Hey, baby," she says to Celia, her voice quivering. "It's okay, you can come in." Ellie tries to smile but her lips look stretched and tight. She gestures to Celia. Then she convulses into a round of violent dry heaves. Celia inches toward the dresser, the bag dangling.

Ellie's head scarf is on crookedly and as she's heaving, it falls into the pan. Gerard puts his hand on Celia's back and maneuvers her out of the room.

"It's going to be okay, sweetheart," he says to her, crouching down to smooth her hair out of her face. She doesn't look upset. The look in her dark eyes isn't childlike at all, but jaded and distrustful. Celia jerks her shoulders and edges away from him. She's holding the bag so tightly it looks like it's going to pop.

"Let's put the fish in the kitchen. We'll acclimate him." Gerard stands, puts a hand on the thin bone of her shoulder, and steers her down the hall. The fish's head looks large—it's the way she's squeezing the bag. He pulls a Tupperware container out of the drawer and fills it with tap water, holds it out to her. She sets the bag into it.

"This way he won't be shocked when we put him in new water," Gerard says. Celia chews on the inside of her cheek and watches the bag float. "Can you entertain yourself for a bit, Bean? I'm going to go help Mommy." Celia shrugs. What's with her shrugging lately? Every question seems to get one.

"I'm traumatizing her," Ellie says when he comes back in the room. Tissues are wadded everywhere, collecting in the spaces between pillows. He takes the pan away and goes into their bathroom to wash it out. The counter is littered with orange bottles. There's an amazing variety; he has no idea how Ellie keeps track of them. She'd better keep her acuity for a while longer because there's no way he'll remember the order, the right amount of pain medicine, steroids, blood cell enhancers, anti-inflammatories, anxiety pills, antidepressants, sleeping pills . . . Jesus. He wets a washcloth and goes out to sit next to her. He puts his hand on her greasy hair and strokes it as she stares dumbly at the wall.

This round, she's been able to keep her hair. One of the drugs a few months back made it fall out and it grew back grayish and curly. Sometimes he looks at her, her hair in corkscrews, short, wiry, and uneven (it never quite came back at her crown), her face puffy and pale, her skin starting to hang off her body—though she's only thirty-six, too young for this sort of age, and he doesn't recognize her. She's a reminder of Ellie, like someone with the same manner in a crowded restaurant.

It's hard not to imagine her dead—even now, running his fingers along her warm scalp, her rib cage expanding with her breath, her face damp, her fingers pressing into his leg—he feels her growing stiff. Sometimes at night he wakes up, certain that the time has come, that she's stopped breathing. There's something amazing about it—the way he rises out of himself, riding a tide of awe—and fear, too, but mostly awe. He feels relief when he puts his hands on her hot face but also dread that this will continue, on and on, that he will wake up every night of his life thinking about death—and the selfishness of this thought dissolves the dread into shame.

"Oh," Ellie says. She lays her head back against the pillow. "Oh. Fuck. The twisting again."

"Can I get you anything?" Gerard says.

"No," Ellie says. "I think I just need to rest."

Ellie decorated the living room. Gerard stares at the abstract painting above the mantel—an odd choice for Ellie, who usually preferred nature prints and antique photographs. The colors—big strokes of olive and gray, red bleeding out of dark spaces, made the piece look brooding. But the rest of the room is cluttered with Ellie's grandmother's basket collection and two old rocking horses, piles of blankets, pillows, magazines. Everything in this house has Ellie's stamp on it; Gerard never cared for decorating. And when she's gone, Gerard imagines that all these objects will cry out for her, like dogs abandoned in a field. He'll have to get rid of everything—right down to the royal blue duvet that she bought him one winter when he complained the old comforter was too small. And then what will he do? Move himself and Celia to the backyard? Spend a year in a tent?

There's a knock at the door and the sound rescues Gerard from what would surely have become a stupor on the sofa.

"Hi, dear," Marsha says, leaning over to kiss his cheek. She smells strongly of vanilla and the blood rushes to his head. She wears her gardening clothes—dirty jeans and a white tank top. Her red bra straps peek out, bright against her freckled shoulders. She's brought a wide-lipped fishbowl—not what Gerard expected. It's low and large and looks like someone sat on it while the glass was cooling. It's full of peaches.

"I stopped by the farmers' market on my way," she says,

walking past him, into the house. Celia appears in the hallway.

"Celia, baby!" Marsha says theatrically. She stops, props the bowl on her hip. A small bit of her side shows where the tank top lifts. "How are things?"

"Okay," Celia says, shifting her weight to one foot. She's gripping a pad of paper and from her back hangs an empty backpack; it's unzipped and the flap hangs down. "I'm kind of busy, though."

"Well, don't let me interfere," Marsha says and winks.

Celia disappears into her bedroom. Gerard follows Marsha into the kitchen.

"That fish is ugly," she says, peering at the bag. She runs water over the peaches.

"Celia chose it," he says. Marsha shakes her head.

"How's Ellie?" she asks. Her short hair is glossy and mussed. She's growing it out, she claims, and so she keeps the sides pinned up in funny bobby pins. Today they have little pink daisies glued to them.

"She's having a bad day," Gerard says. He walks up behind her, too close; he can feel the warmth of her body through her clothes. The vanilla is mixed with another smell, something warm and magnetic, almost spicy. He presses his nose against the side of her head. She keeps rinsing the peaches, but he can feel the tension shooting through her. He's encouraged and puts his hand on her ass, slides it down between her legs.

"Should we bring some of these in for her?" Marsha asks. "We could cut them and put a little yogurt in a dish." She reaches up to the shelf next to the sink for one of Ellie's handmade bowls and he can't resist, he slips his hand under her shirt and turns her around to face him. She leans away and looks at him with that familiar danger in her eyes, coy and a little cold. He kisses her, openmouthed and sloppy; she runs her fingertips down his chest.

"Not right now," she whispers, and he untangles himself. She turns back around and opens the silverware drawer.

"Hey, sugar," Marsha says, sitting on the side of the bed.

"Hi, Marsh." Ellie's still propped on the pillows but it's clear she's been dozing. The room smells sharply of bile and old sweat. "What did you bring me?" she asks. She raises her hands to her hair and smooths it with an expert caress; it's a gesture left over from the old Ellie, the pretty, vain Ellie with a long mane of shockingly blond ringlets. On the new Ellie it looks wrong, a grotesque impersonation. She pulls the cover up to her armpits and holds it there.

"I stopped at the market," Marsha says. "You wouldn't believe who I saw with Dale Kerchaw, that pig." Ellie's face lights up. Marsha sets the yogurt and peaches on the nightstand and straightens the stack of magazines. "That twenty-two-year-old nurse!"

Gerard backs out of the room to let them gossip. He knocks softly on Celia's door.

"Come in," she calls. She's sitting on the floor with eight dolls lined up on folded blankets or towels. None of them have any clothes on.

"What're you up to?" Gerard asks.

"I'm playing," she says. In her hands she's got a ballpoint pen and she looks a little guilty. He walks toward her and kneels.

"What are you playing?"

"Hospital," she says. "They're sick." And then Gerard sees that a bunch of the dolls have little holes in their arms, pressed into the plastic or cloth with the pen. The holes are small, black with ink around the edges.

"Why are you sticking them with a pen?" he asks, pressing his hands against a creepy-looking brunette, its blue eyes trained at the ceiling.

"I'm helping them," she says.

Gerard waits. He's sure he will start to feel something. He looks at his daughter. Her dark eyes seem misplaced in her pale face. She has almost no lashes, no eyebrows, and yet she has his eyes, dark and large, and his oversized lips. She's not pretty, though it's not clear why. All her features are handsome but they're poorly combined. There's something fishlike about her, actually.

"Isn't there another game you could play?" Gerard asks. Celia looks at him gravely and shrugs.

Why is it that no one around here can get enough of death? Even Marsha comes up to see Ellie almost every day. And though it's terribly kind, gives Ellie something to look forward to and gives Gerard a chance for carnal release—he can't help but wonder sometimes if she's a little bit attracted to the spectacle of decline. It's more excruciating and exhilarating than any carnival ride or horror film. It's happening right in front of them, what they all fear most.

Gerard stands up. "Maybe we should go put the fish in the bowl Marsha brought."

"Can you just do it?" Celia asks, twirling her pen. "I don't want to."

Outside her window, he can see the sun reflecting off

Marsha's red car. They'd had sex in that car on Thursday. They'd driven out to look at the flower farms, to pick Ellie daisies and irises, and had parked on the side of a dirt road afterward, the flowers wrapped in paper, flung all over the backseat. Marsha leaned over the emergency brake and unbuttoned his pants. He was already hard when she ran her tongue down him, wedged her fingers below his balls. And then, as if they were still sixteen, she crawled over him, lifted her long, flowery skirt, slid her underwear off until it hung from one knee, and jerkily fit him inside of her.

She came so easily. It was nothing like Ellie. He had to work for Ellie's pleasure. He had to go down on her, play with her, watch her arch and tense and then lose her focus, bring her back to center, keep the rhythm going. That was how it used to be, anyway. He hadn't had sex with Ellie in almost a year. They'd tried a few times, but it was so depressing. She couldn't get into it, all the smells were off, and it ended in tears. Marsha did this thing with her hips and ass, pressing herself away from him a little, jerking angrily, and then she just came, loudly, unexpectedly, expelling air and noise like a sea mammal, her small eyes glittery and distant.

Gerard shoves his hands in his pockets. Celia is waiting for him to leave. He bites his bottom lip and feels a worm of longing roll inside of him.

Celia looks down at her dolls, her posture full of purpose, and punctures another one with her pen.

Gerard rinses out the squashed-looking bowl and fills it with the water from the container. He takes the bag and undoes the rubber band. The fish isn't looking at him. The fish is darting back and forth in the bag like it's looking for a corner.

One of these days, Ellie's going to slip into a coma. That's how it happens. Or for some reason that's what Gerard has decided. One day he's going to walk into the bedroom with a cup of tea and she's going to be staring glassily at the ceiling, just like that doll. He'll sit calmly on the bed with her, repeating her name. And then he'll call Marsha and the two of them will call the ambulance together—they'll watch as Ellie's loaded in, wrapped in her favorite afghan, the one her great-grandmother knit in stripes of avocado and red—and the doctors will admit her so she can have the right doses of things—or so she can have an IV bag, at least. And he and Marsha will sit vigilantly in a small, medicinal room, breathing in molecules of bodies on their way to becoming dust—and they will look at each other, he and Marsha, and sometimes they'll go back to her tiny house and eat cottage cheese with salsa and fuck in her cramped bedroom, both of them nauseated with lack of sleep, and people will probably send flowers, Ellie's obese sister Petra will probably show up, bearing some awful food for him, sausage lasagna or beef stew. And Celia will be home with a sitter. And sometimes he will bring Celia to the hospital. And that's how the end will be.

There's moisture around the top of the bag and Gerard moves his thumb and forefinger together so that the two plastic sheets slide pleasurably between them. The fish catches light from the window on its scales and shines through the murky water. Does it know that it's about to begin a lifelong incarceration? That it will swim in circles every day of its life? Or does the fish just exist for the moment—and what would that be like—to live every moment with no concept of past or future? If he could exist only in this moment, then he'd see only the fish and the water and the dirt particles and the light. He would feel that he tied his left sneaker too tight and that it's cutting off some circulation in his foot. He wouldn't think of Ellie's ravaged body—the smell of decay when you got close to her—sweet and fishy. He wouldn't remember what it was like before she got sick. How they used to collapse next to each other on the sofa after work and complain. God! What had they complained about? And he really did like the challenge of Ellie's body then—the way he had to work to bring her over the edge, to distract her from the stress of her mind, and then when he finally did, she shook and would hold on to him afterward, her long fingers kneading his while she dozed.

And then—shit! He's still holding the bag, but only one side of it, and there's water all over the floor, cascading off the counter, running down toward his feet. The fish is on the counter, flopping toward the edge in small, spastic jerks. He reaches for the tail, but it slips through his fingers. Dammit! He tries again. The fish is slick, muscular. It can't die. No! Not in this house, nothing else is going to die! It's cold and orange and has no pigment on one side, that's why Celia liked it. The fish between his fingers feels like something internal—something he has no right to be touching—and his insides get hot and his joints feel shaky but he pinches down hard and moves fast and manages to get the fish back in the stupid bowl.

"Fuck you," Gerard says to it. And then he turns to see if anyone has seen him. But he's alone in the kitchen, the bright blue wall, the white shelves, the glass jars full of herbs turning gray in the sun.

Gerard starts to tremble a little and a pain shoots from his back to his head. His heart pounds furiously. He's dizzy. The room gets brighter, slowly brighter—but not that slowly. The edges of the counter are getting so bright they're fading out. He's not okay. He's going to collapse. He's going to die and die first! He's sweating now, and this takes all of his strength. He has to sit. His knees give gently, it's as though large hands are pushing him down, and then he's on all fours. He's spinning, an ax is banging on the bone of his forehead from the inside and something is too hot inside of him. He can't breathe and his heart is pounding and his saliva is doing something weird—he can taste his saliva. As soon as he can stand up again, as soon as he stops tasting this—so bitter, like a plant he shouldn't be chewing on—as soon as he can breathe again he'll knock that fish onto the floor and he will be able to breathe because—he thinks—something will be let go, the soul of the fish will be let go.

Gerard sweats, a bead of it falls onto the parquet floors, his hand turns white from pressing down, his body spins and spins and there is Celia. She is talking to him, she is running toward the bedroom—

And he should take the fish outside because its soul might get caught against the ceiling and hover and maybe he should make Ellie die outside too because her soul might get trapped in the house and then they would have to move, but how could they sell the house to someone knowing Ellie's soul was caught in it? He's trying to get himself outside, scooting on his arms, trying to get toward the front parlor so he can die outside—they are all going to die outside, this is the only thing that makes any sense. This makes *sense*. Ha! He's going to die *first*! And then there are hands on his back, grabbing him by the waist of his pants. What on earth, Marsha is saying, Gerard, get a hold of yourself but he can't breathe—he's laughing! And there is Ellie, teary and odd-looking, holding on to the wall. He can see right through her. Ha ha ha ha! HA! He is going to die first and that will be something! Something no one could have expected.

It's the Xanax that Marsha gets from Ellie's stash that finally calms him. Marsha sets him up in the living room and turns on cartoons—a cat racing through a well-manicured forest. He feels so light. He feels so good, actually. Like his thoughts have been bleached and fluffed.

"Come sit with me," he says. Ellie's gone back to the bedroom. Marsha squints at him.

"I don't think that's such a good idea," she says.

"Just come here," he says, patting the cushion.

Marsha reluctantly sets her bag down. When she sits, she's stiff, her legs bent in ninety-degree angles, her feet parallel. Gerard wants to laugh. She looks like a diagram!

He puts his face against her chest. She stiffens even more and pushes it away.

"Not now," she says. "Gerard, get a grip."

He leans away from her. Her face puckers, her eyes scrunch.

"Marsha," he says, reaching out for her shoulders.

"What the hell," Marsha hisses, slapping his hands away. "What are you doing? What was all that?" She stands. He can hear her shoes clack as she stalks down the hall. The front door opens, slams. He would chase her, but his body doesn't feel like it could move that fast. His shirt feels fuzzy and warm.

The clatter of pans wakes him. It's dark out now. Dread hits him as soon as he's conscious, before he even remembers what happened. He stands and his knees crack. They're sore.

Ellie's in the kitchen. She's dressed in her nice clothes—her red washed-silk pants and an orange cashmere sweater; he hasn't seen these clothes in so long. They went to an opera once—Celia was smaller then, maybe six—and Ellie wore that sweater. Her hair is damp from a shower. She turns to look at him, her face pale and serious.

Gerard looks at the wall clock. It's ten-thirty. Shit, he didn't make Celia dinner and now she must be asleep.

Ellie has a large pot on the stove.

"What are you doing?" he asks. She's put on makeup and you can't tell she's dying—not really. The eye shadow glimmers up to her eyebrow.

"I'm making soup. We didn't have a lot of stuff, but there were dried lentils and that beef shank in the freezer. And Marsha brought all those carrots."

Ellie hasn't cooked in two months, not since the pain got so bad she had to take pills on top of the pain patch. She barely has the energy to get back and forth from the bedroom to the living room to watch an hour of television. He stands next to her. She's wearing perfume, dark, leathery, and woodsy. Small circles of carrots line the cutting board; the lentils boil, filling the room with their bean smell.

He looks at the fish. It swims in circles, flipping its body around and around. He takes the yellow container of fish food Marsha brought and shakes some into the water. The fish darts up and sucks the flakes down.

Ellie sets down the knife and holds out her arms to him. Beneath the orange cashmere those arms are so thin, bruised from various injections.

"I'm so sorry, sweetheart," she says. She's crying. Soon they'll all cry so much they'll flood the house; they'll damage the foundation. She's shaking her head. The mascara leaves speckled tracks down her cheeks.

He walks over to her, takes her body. *Ellie,* he wants to say—just her name. The lentils roll over themselves, making a soft sound. The fish hovers at the top of the bowl. Nothing else in the room moves. He's gripping her too tightly; he can feel her tensing away. But it's all he can do. He can't let go.

THE MOTHER GARDEN

AUREL'S THE NEWEST ARRIVAL. SHE WON'T BEHAVE.

"Don't put me next to Agnes," she says. "That heifer."

"That's mean," I tell Laurel as I jam her feet into the tilled soil. Her kitten heels make good digging tools and I'm able to get her wedged in deep.

"I've worked hard for this figure," Laurel says. "And I'll be damned if I get stuck beside all the fat I've left behind." Agnes smoothes her dress over her stomach and thighs. The breeze blows a few of her brown curls loose from her barrette.

"Agnes's curves are part of her charm," I say.

"You mean Agnes's curves belong in a barn," Laurel says. Her eyes glint like sun on metal.

"You're being a bitch," I say to Laurel. The other mothers pretend not to notice. "I'm sorry, Agnes."

*　　*　　*

I can't take credit for the garden, not entirely. It was Jack's idea. We were having beers after work a few months ago and he'd just talked to his mother. His face, always prone to pinkness, was nearly violet.

"I've been calling her once a week, you know, to forge a relationship, and she has *never* asked me about my life. I'm not exaggerating. She just goes *on* and *on*." Jack's voice went up a few octaves. " *'Maryanne's getting remarried to that nice man at the post office, you remember, Dudley Bilson— you played horseshoes at his house. And Boz Parker ran off with that little blonde he just hired, Connie is just a wreck. You should see her, Jack, she looks terrible.' "* I pushed some foam around the top of my glass. As a general rule, people don't complain to me about their mothers. "She would keep going for hours if I didn't interrupt her," he said. "You have no idea, Claire, you just don't." Jack picked up his coaster and started tapping it on the table. "It's shitty of me to be ungrateful, I know, you're going to play the dead mom card."

"Maybe you could loan her out," I said. "I might borrow her." For a moment Jack was still, his little beard a handle pulling his mouth open.

"Maybe there's something to that," he said, and jotted an idea on a bar napkin.

Jack's a landscape designer. He did the sloping gardens at the university—dark purple foliage and bright green flowers. That garden has made its way into magazines and design shows, everything a little off-kilter. We've been best friends since our failed love affair in college. I've seen him rise through the ranks, from weekend gardener to Master of Landscape Architecture. Now I'm collaborating with him to stretch the frontier of landscaping. He expands his portfolio and I get all the moms I've missed. We're blending land and family. We're altering space and our conceptions of the garden. We're cutting edge.

It was easy to get Jack's mom, Doreena, to volunteer. She retired two years ago from her job with the postal service and shortly thereafter, her dog died of lupus. Jack is her only child. She doesn't hear a word he says, but she'd do anything for him.

We installed Doreena on a Saturday afternoon. She sat on the grass and held out her bunioned feet as if for a pedicure. Jack carefully settled them into the hole. He filled a bucket with warm water and poured it over her feet, then packed the dirt around her ankles. Doreena squared her meaty shoulders; her russet hair stood straight from her head like quills.

"She looks magical out there," Jack remarked that evening as we watched her from the kitchen window. We'd put Doreena near the back fence and the bougainvillea rose up behind her, framing her stout figure in blobs of purple. The moonlight spilled off the leaves and gutters, tinting her skin a milky blue.

"Do you think she'll get bored?" I asked.

Jack shrugged. "She does a bang-up job talking to herself," he said. "It seems to keep her busy."

That night I tried to sleep, but each time I'd drift, Doreena's voice would break the silence.

"Goodness!" she said. "You are an ugly bug! You go back to your ugly bug world!"

At three in the morning, I opened my window.

"Doreena," I called.

"Yes, dear?"

"Do you think you could keep it down?"

"Oh!" she said. "I didn't realize I was talking."

My mother has been dead for more than a decade. My memories of her feel static. They're like film clips that I play over and over: my mother sitting at the kitchen table with her brown ceramic mug, her dark curls clasped in a leaf-shaped clip. She says, "Claire-belle, look at the magnolia tree." Her face looks dreamy. "I was twenty-three before I saw anything that pretty." Or: she sits by the side of my bed, her feet gauzy in nylons. A bowl of broth steams on the old wooden tray. "If you want, there're noodles in the kitchen," she says. Her cool hand sweeps over my damp forehead. "Poor babe," she says. "You look like a noodle."

It's been a long time without her now—almost as long without her as with her.

"Mom," I sometimes say to the dirt, to the tree, to the old recycle bin, "that was a dumb time to go." The recycle bin sits blue and still. The dirt stares back at me with its dark face. The tree sways in the wind.

"I'm not sure I can deal," I said to Jack the next morning when he stopped by on his way to work. "I slept for three hours. She talks incessantly."

Jack looked at me in faux shock. "Not *my* mother!" he said, helping himself to some coffee and a banana. He peeled it while watching Doreena from the window. She was asking and answering questions about the weather.

"You get used to it," he said.

That day, Jack put an ad online and an hour later, we got a reply. "Namaste," it read. "My name is Erika and I'm looking for community, ultimate peace, and belonging. And a place to stay."

"She sounds ideal," Jack said when I told him.

Erika arrived the following morning, free of material possessions, her posture perfect. I showed her the garden, she admired the bougainvillea and trumpet vine, the huge St. John's wort, the window box of herbs.

"What a beautiful space," she said slowly.

Doreena waved. "Hi there," she trilled. "Over here the sun's just right. When I was a little girl, my brother Moe and I, bless his heart, used to sit outside to see whose hair got hotter first. He always won, of course, that Moe. He was a brunette." She held out her hand. Instead of taking it, Erika placed her palms together in front of her heart and bowed her head.

"That's *different,*" Doreena said, smiling so wide we could see the gray sealant on one of her molars. "I like that." She put her hands together too and showed us the top of her head, the scalp discolored from hair dye.

Jack arrived in his work clothes, looking harried and annoyed. (He'd wanted to schedule the meeting after he got off, but Erika had a ride at ten.) He gave his mom a halfhearted hug. But when he saw Erika's long neck and soft mouth, he perked up. He walked her around the garden, explaining our vision: mothers bursting out of the earth alongside other stalwart flora, lush and abundant. Erika nodded gravely after every sentence.

"So, the one criteria is that you're a mother," Jack finished. Erika wove her fingers together and sat on the porch steps.

"I'm not focusing on that part of my life these days," she said. "I try to orient toward joy." Jack sat next to her and made his forehead soft. In an instant he could go from brusque to sensitive, as open as a daisy in the sunshine. Erika opened her nostrils and breathed deeply, letting the air slowly out of her mouth.

"When I was seventeen," she said (she couldn't have been older than twenty-four), "I did a few things I'm not that proud of." I looked over at Doreena, who, uncharacteristically quiet, pretended to study the hem of her Hilton Head sweatshirt. Erika glanced over at her. "I gave them up." Jack tilted his head, nodded slowly.

"More than one?" he asked.

It looked as though she'd turned to glass. "Twins," Erika said.

"Welcome," Jack said, plucking a ranunculus from the planter box. She melted toward him, took the flower, and wove it into her waist-length hair.

We planted Erika near my bedroom window so that in the morning, when she did yoga, I could see her stretch into the sky as though plucking a cloud.

Contrary to our expectations, Erika and Doreena balanced nicely. Doreena rambled all day—people she'd known, pets she saw once, the formidable diabetes problem—and Erika meditated.

I brought them their meals each day and tried to engage them.

"How was your night?" I'd ask. Invariably, Doreena would recall a story she heard on a talk show about a woman who spent nine months in the woods with only a jackknife. "She was so *tan*!" Or she might repeat how lucky she was that, at her age, she hadn't suffered any sig-

nificant bone loss according to her doctor. Erika would
zone out and stare at the eaves.

Even with Erika and Doreena's yin-yang effect, there
was something depressing about having only two mothers
in a garden. I didn't want to burst Jack's bubble, but without a few more moms, they just looked like women in a
yard, their ankles packed in dirt. I reposted Jack's ad daily
on various sites. For almost a week, no one else responded.

"It's not going to work," I told Jack. We were sitting on
my sofa watching a gardening show. He ate a handful of
popcorn. "There's no incentive."

"Don't be negative," he said. "Big ideas take a while to
catch. Besides, look." He pulled out a piece of tagboard
from his bag. On it were patches of oil paint in earthy
shades of brown, purple, peach, and faded indigo. "I did the
color scheme," he said. "It's great, right?" He ran his thumb
over the colors. "Beauty is its own incentive, Claire."

That week, Jack convinced Doreena to grow out her
dye job, explaining that the white in her hair would more
dramatically reflect light. He brought over a black cocktail
dress for Erika, but when she put it on and stood ankle
deep in soil, she looked out of place, like a girl stumbling
from a car crash. Instead he settled on a loose silk dress in
a loamy brown. Every couple of days he brought over small
purple flowers for her hair. He seemed to take special care
with Erika, going so far as to buy her a sparkly body spray
that smelled like wood.

But still, no more mothers responded. I took out a small
ad in the local paper. When that didn't work, I decided to
make fliers. *Don't make art, BE art! Join The Mother Garden! All mothers encouraged to inquire!* Jack's drawing of the
project sat beneath the text, all the flowers carefully

sketched. The silhouettes of the mothers he left white—beautiful and strange.

All day I walked the city, hanging the flier outside day care centers and malls, clothing boutiques and grocery stores. As I was putting the stapler back in my bag at the natural grocery, a woman stopped to read it. Two young boys stood in her grocery cart alongside bags of produce and packages of dried fruit. The woman's eyebrows arched over plastic European glasses. She probably sang her sons lullabies in French and cut strawberries into their cereal in the morning. She'd correct their pronunciation and tap their shoulders when they slumped. As the boys grew older, they'd roll their eyes and snort, but secretly they'd search all their lives for women just like her.

She'd be perfect for the garden—her slim physique and interesting bone structure. We'd probably have things in common, too. I took French in college. I'd traveled a bit. I waited to see if she'd take a phone number.

The bigger boy looked me straight in the eye. Then he made his hand into a claw and slammed it into his brother's nose. The smaller boy became entirely mouth: dark, cavernous, tinseled with spit. He wailed.

"Jonah!" the mother said. "You say you're sorry *right* now!" Then she looked at me, pushing her glasses up.

"Intriguing flier," she said. She rolled her eyes and gestured to her son. "As if any mother has time for games." She smiled sympathetically at me, as if I couldn't help drooling on myself. Then she wheeled her cart over to a rack of organic peach nectar. Her older son turned to face me. He bugged his eyes and opened his mouth wide like a bat.

I left feeling low. It wasn't just for me, the garden. It

was for the great frontier of art. I knew that my mother was dead. This wasn't simply a monument to the past. But maybe it was too bizarre; maybe I should call it off, send them home. It would piss off Jack, but it really wasn't up to him. It was my yard.

I pushed open the side gate.

"Hi there, Claire," Doreena called. Erika stood with her eyes shut. In between them, midway across the mulch, another woman stood.

"I hope I'm in a good spot," she said, glancing around. She'd already planted herself; you could see part of her muscular calves beneath her long orange skirt. "It seemed like the best place for me." Her face was doll-like, a peaked nose and knobby chin. I walked over. Her spot was notably cooler than the other spots, cast in the shed's shadow.

"I'm Agnes." She offered her hand. On her right pinky sat an enormous garnet. As she extended it, all the light from the sky was swallowed by that stone.

My mother's mother had a garnet ring, the color of almost dry blood. When my grandmother died, my mother had it made into a pendant. I remember a particular outfit she wore: a black tunic with a full black skirt, black ballet flats, and the glossy red pendant displayed prominently against her sternum. At night she kept the garnet in a satin-lined brass box. The day we buried her, I stood by the grave, watching people's shoes as they shifted their weight. The dirt fell on the pine box with a hollow thump, and then, as dirt hit dirt, it made no sound at all. The adults passed the shovel as the rabbi keened. All these people would follow us back to the house, eat tuna salad and bagels and drink fruity soda as they talked. When they left, I planned to go into her bedroom, where her garnet would be cool and smooth.

But when I got to her room, the brass box was empty. My father and I tore the house apart looking for the pendant. In the middle of the night I came downstairs to find him on his hands and knees with a flashlight, peering around the shoes in my mother's closet. "I can't understand it," he said to me, his voice shrill, his face ashen. His wrists looked very thin.

That evening, I took them a little champagne to celebrate Agnes. Her presence out back made a significant difference.

"So, where are your children?" I asked her. She made a fluttering motion with her hand.

"Oh, grown and flown, dear," she said. "My daughter's married and living in Idaho. My son's in graduate school in Montreal." She handed me her empty glass. "Do you have a sweater I could use for the night?" she asked. "I know I'm not your size, exactly, but I didn't think to bring one."

The small attic of my house contained nothing but boxes of my mom's things. Dishes and figurines, her wedding dress. I dragged one down labeled CLOTHES. When Agnes put on the crimson pullover, it fit her perfectly.

One afternoon Agnes told Erika that she should try to write to her children, even if she couldn't send the letters. "Start with getting your thoughts straight," she advised. Erika ripped a buttercup to shreds as Agnes talked, but the next day she asked for some paper and a pen. Agnes had a calming effect on Doreena. She still chattered, but with Agnes around there were periods of time when she'd look at the trees or examine her lunch basket without sharing her observations.

My enthusiasm for the project intensified. In the mornings I brought the mothers coffee (Erika drank green tea), and Agnes and I would chat. She asked me questions about where I grew up and when I told her about my mother, she pressed on her collarbone so as not to cry.

Jack asked me to type a sample press release. We weren't quite ready to open to the public, but he thought if we could get one or two more mothers in the next week, we could do a preliminary showing. I fussed with it after breakfast, then I made Erika's recipe for cream cheese sandwiches with pimento-pistachio paste. I handed them to the mothers in napkins. I was headed to Jack's, to print out what I'd written, when I heard yelling.

Agnes must have torn herself from the dirt in a hurry. Clumps stuck to her ankles. She rummaged through the first aid box Jack fastened to the wall of the shed, and rushed to Doreena. She yanked Doreena's slacks down and slammed her clenched fist against her dappled thigh. Doreena's hands fell away from her throat.

"It's okay," Agnes said. Erika, who'd just begun to dig herself up, stopped moving. Agnes pulled up Doreena's pants. With maternal grace, she dusted off the mulch.

"What happened?" I asked.

"She didn't realize there were nuts in the sandwich. She's allergic," Agnes said.

"Oh, Doreena." I walked down the wooden steps into the garden. "I didn't know. I'm sorry."

That night, Jack and I installed a small clay fireplace by the back fence while the moms soaked their dirty feet in basins of sudsy water. We brought out bags of marshmallows and chocolate. Jack played simple songs on his new mandolin. Doreena sat silently and at one point in the evening, Jack put his arm around her.

We replanted the moms in their spots around midnight, toasting their magnificence with jars of hot toddies.

"Where would we be without you?" I said to Agnes. Her hair fell just like my mother's, dark and incorrigible, all over her face. She reached out and touched my shoulder.

"You can't save everyone," she said softly. "But you save who you can."

"What's the matter with you, anyway?" Laurel hisses at Agnes. "How hard is it to diet? For Pete's sake, couldn't you get a little cardio every once in a while?" Laurel's dangerously thin. You can see the strap of muscle coil around her upper arm, the tendons in her neck. When you get too close to her, she smells sulfuric.

Agnes doesn't respond. It's a ridiculous attack. She's not fat, though her body has more curves than the other mothers. Her breasts are formidable and her hips make her long skirt bell.

"I would appreciate it if you'd keep your opinions to yourself," Agnes says.

"I would appreciate it if you'd move your big ass," Laurel says.

"Watch your language," Doreena says.

Erika turns to Laurel. "You're a little out of line," she says.

"You're a little out of touch," Laurel shoots back. "That long hair thing went out with Crystal Gayle in, like, nineteen seventy-nine." For a moment Erika looks wounded. Her long fingers rise to touch her tresses, but then she stops.

"It must be difficult being you," she says.

"Not at all," Laurel says. "It's fantastic." She begins a series of squats.

A ladybug lands on Agnes's sweater. It crawls over her breasts and into the crease of her armpit. She inserts a finger into the crease and the glossy bug crawls onto it.

"Three spots, three wishes," Agnes says, handing the bug to me. It sits on my finger. I'm always tempted to wish for things I cannot have—*I wish there were no such thing as loss*—but before I can think of a better wish, it flies off into the bougainvillea.

Laurel is mother number four. For her I got twenty grand. Jack landscaped the yard at her husband Franz's law firm and the two of them got to talking about the mother garden. Because Franz is a lawyer and the garden is technically mine, the offer (on creamy cotton paper) came addressed to me. Laurel needed something to do— the acting wasn't panning out; he needed space to focus on the office remodel. Their kids were in high school, able to get themselves to basketball and sailing club. He'd pay me the money for her upkeep and in addition, he'd throw in a weekly hairstylist and a biweekly shrink.

"What do you think?" I asked Jack.

"I think we're going to get a call from Montel Williams any second."

"Or Jerry Springer," I said

"Maybe Martha Stewart," he said. I thought of all the projects we could put in *Living*. A mom bouquet with colorful streamers around it. Sunhats full of birdseed to attract the jays. On weekends we could invite motherless girls to make gingerbread houses with the mom of their choice.

"Twenty grand," Jack said. "We'd be crazy to pass that up."

"Do you think I should go over and meet her?"

"Chh," Jack said. "If you can deal with Doreena, you can deal with some retired trophy wife."

Laurel hasn't stopped moving since she arrived. Her arms spiral, her fanny wags, she does a hundred squats at a time. She won't eat anything but lettuce and celery. Her limp blond hair is ragged at the tips. She looks like a malnourished daffodil.

"You spray me with that hose and I'll scream," Laurel yells. Something's stuck a little farther up the hose than I can reach. I've forced a twig down to dislodge it. It seems plausible that Laurel stuck gum in there. She's always chewing it. "You seem to be on some kind of power trip, missy, but you're just a pipsqueak with this bizarre fetish. And when my agent gets wind of this, boy—"

I finally get the thing out of the hose. It's not gum, it's a snail, and I've broken its dark little shell. I aim the strong spray at Laurel's bony legs. The tension jangles Doreena, who immediately starts to recount various supersales at Marshall's. For half an hour, from the kitchen, I can hear Laurel's litigation threats mingling with bargain prices.

"Don't talk to me," I say to Laurel when I go back outside. Agnes looks defeated. She sits with her ankles in the dirt, knees clasped. She looks at me, waiting.

"We'll figure this out," I tell her. "I'm sure she'll calm down after a day or two."

"A day or two?" Agnes says, shaking her head. "I'm sorry, Claire, but I'm afraid this isn't what I came here for. I'm not up for it."

"Wait," I say. I put my hand on her shoulder.

"Claire?" she says, reaching up to touch my hand. It's then I realize how hard I'm squeezing.

*   *   *

I never thought through losing these moms. Jack and I figured we'd max out at ten, get a lot of publicity, and maybe buy a larger piece of land where we could expand. He sees us landing an NEA grant—what with the administration so fixed on family issues. "It's the perfect project," he said. "All happy endings and unity." And the moms would be bountiful. Over the weeks they've been out back, I've slept better. I don't have nightmares of being left in the desert with only a ruler, of being put on a rowboat in a storm with my fingers rotting.

From the kitchen window, I watch them. Laurel's absorbed in a swiveling motion, probably designed to enhance the waistline. Erika rakes her hands through her hair, vacantly studying some grass. Doreena rambles about cholesterol, her eyes wide, the white roots of her hair beginning to show.

I could bring Agnes inside the house. But there's no garden in there—what would I tell the other moms? I could convince her to try a new part of the yard. I could give Franz back his money, though at this point, I see I've been duped. He's not taking Laurel back. *Stay,* I could tell Agnes. *Please. Don't go.*

"Don't go," I said to my mother. She was on the rented hospital bed in the study, a dead plant resting on the table near her feet. I'd killed that plant, withholding water for weeks. I crawled onto the bed when the social worker left the room and straddled her, peeled her eyelids with my thumbs. *"Mom,"* I said. She opened her mouth and a noise like the creak of a door came out. "Mom, you have to open your eyes." Her tongue moved. *"Open your eyes."* And then she did, she looked straight ahead, past me, past the ceiling. *"Look at me,"* I said. "Don't go." My tears hit her lips. Then she rattled, a shake went through her, and she left.

There will be more moms, I tell myself. As soon as our press release hits local papers, the moms will be lining up to join. Look at the trumpet vine, the herb garden, the fireplace. Look at the new dress Jack bought for Agnes. "To accentuate her goddess shape," he'd said. With the cream chiffon she wore green malachite beads and a pale sage belt. She kept the crimson cardigan for the evenings. He'd even given Doreena a new outfit. He chose a soft flame-colored shirt for her that hung below her hips. With it, she wore peach culottes with fine green stitching. It was a beautiful project, our garden. The birds gathered on the roof of the shed, tilting their little heads to the sky as they twittered. Cats from the neighborhood prowled the fences, sunned themselves on the lawn.

Maybe if I gave the moms a unifying project—something to shift their focus. Jack had basic woodworking skills. We could make the back deck bigger, and with the money we got for Laurel we could install one of those wine barrel hot tubs. Then, at night, amidst a tangle of flowering vines, the mothers could soak in the starlight.

I open the refrigerator to get some juice and there she is, my mother, in her dark tunic, the garnet shining against her pale skin. She looks waxy with bright lips and a long, sharp nose.

Claire. Her eyes are fierce. *What are you doing out in that yard? You're acting like a nutcase.*

I try to close the refrigerator but she locks her arm, holds it open.

"What are you doing here?" I say. For a while, after she died, she'd creep into my room some nights, sit quietly on the edge of the bed, touch my hair, but she hasn't bothered to do this in years. "You can't say anything about this!" My words bounce off the appliances. I dig my nails into my arms because pain makes ghosts disappear, but she stays and looks reproachful.

Then the front door opens and a teenage girl flies into the kitchen holding a pink leather purse.

"Where is she?" she says. I look around but my mother is gone. I shut the refrigerator and feel a little shaky. The girl gets right in my face. I smell her soap and perfume mingling, strawberry gum in a violet patch. Makeup cakes her skin, and her brown hair, carefully streaked with blond, sways in a sloppy ponytail.

"What are you, some kind of freak?" she continues. "Totally fucking unbelievable." She jets out back before I can stop her and tugs on Laurel.

"Hey," I yell. "What are you doing!" I rush over to slap her hands away.

"Get the hell away from us!" the girl screams. Laurel smiles smugly.

"This is my daughter, Taylor," Laurel says.

"You can't go," I say to Laurel.

"Watch me," she says. Taylor grabs a nearby spade and begins furiously digging out Laurel's feet. A brown smudge works its way across Taylor's short white skirt. The rest of the moms watch, hushed.

"No, actually, you have to stay," I try again. "It was part of the agreement."

"Oh, really?" Laurel says sharply. "Who exactly agreed?"

Taylor turns to me. "What, are you sleeping with my dad, too? Is that how you got involved? You look just like the last girl—all arty. Give me a break. Your shit stinks, too." And with that, she grabs her mother by the arm and leaves out the side gate.

I walk over to the hole she left and kick some dirt over it. "Good riddance," I say, but the three mothers cast their eyes down. "She was a handful, anyway." Erika takes her hair and twists it into a coil. She tugs on her silk outfit.

"The energy has gotten a little bad around here," she says. She looks at Doreena.

"I'm feeling like a shower at the homestead myself," Doreena says. "All this sun has made me itchy." They both lean down and begin to dig out their legs.

Agnes stands where she started, near the shed. I can feel her watching me. It takes almost no time for the mothers to be unearthed. Doreena retrieves their shoes from the basket by the porch. I shouldn't have left them there.

"Don't be mopey!" Doreena trills. "I'm sure I'll see you again. When I come out next, I'll take you and Jack wherever you'd like to eat. Maybe we can even try that place that Erika told me about. It sounded *different*." She accidentally hits the bougainvillea with her elbow and her shirt gets caught on a thorn. Erika walks over and unhooks it.

"It's only raw food," Erika clarifies. Then she adds, "This may be my real good-bye. I'm interested in checking out that ashram in Oregon."

Doreena props the gate open with her white sneaker. Erika leans down and tugs some crabgrass out from the mulch and tucks it in her pocket.

"Are you sticking around?" she asks Agnes. Agnes shrugs.

The other mothers have left small disturbances in the mulch, little holes. All by herself, Agnes looks strange, standing knee deep in soil in the middle of the yard. She puts a hand on her hip and the garnet winks.

"I'll stay for a bit," she says. "At least for dinner."

The house is very still.

"Your mom escaped," I tell Jack's voice mail. "And she took Erika. And Laurel's been—stolen." I wait for the right words to come—words that match the dark heavy feeling. The recorder beeps.

Out my bedroom window, I watch Agnes pick at a hangnail. Later I order Chinese for dinner and take her a plate.

The grass smells rich and sweet and we sit together in silence, eating.

"Why did you let them all go?" Agnes asks. She's eyeing me with those wise eyes. Her fingers are oily. A little bit of cabbage sticks to her lip.

"I didn't let them, they just went."

"You let them go," Agnes said. "You didn't run after them."

"What good would it have done?" I take a piece of roast duck from a box and begin to peel off the skin. "You can't hold things against their will," I say.

"Isn't that Zen of you," Agnes says. "Are you forgetting about zoos and jails?"

"This wasn't supposed to be a zoo."

"What is it then?"

"A garden," I say.

Agnes reaches over and as soon as her fingers make

contact I feel like I've swallowed a sting. She strokes my hair and her ring gets caught for a moment. I pull away.

"Claire-belle," she croons. "You're a little confused." I can't breathe.

She's not there. I try to conjure her image on the backs of my eyelids—waxy skin, red lips, the sheen of her pendant—but I can't do it. She won't come. And when I open my eyes, Agnes is all I see. The blood of her stone, her dark curls, her crooning.

FAMILY EPIC

It's not the first time my grandmother's come, falling through the ceiling the way she does. This time she arrives just after my father calls to ask if he can stop by around dinnertime with his new girlfriend, Ariella. My grandmother takes off her plastic rain cap and instead of the red dye job—always jarring on her angled, olive face— her gray hair tumbles down her back. She tosses her vinyl handbag on the table and takes off her coat. She wears nothing but a slip.

Ariella, my father's new flame, is my age, twenty-nine to his sixty. She and I went to junior high together. And though everyone says it has been three years now, he should get *back in the saddle,* I'd prefer he continue to stand next to the horse.

"I'm waiting for a call," my grandmother says, blocking the phone. She holds up her gnarled hand. On it is the ring she always wore, the ring we have stored in a locked box at the bank. It's a tulip made from tiny specks of diamond set flatly into white gold, the size of a dandelion, large for a ring. Her body is old; I can see her breasts stretched toward her navel, used-looking. But her face is the face of a girl. Her lips are painted opaque pink, her lids are smeared with blue. Around her neck hangs a tangle of gold chains.

How my father hated her. After she died, ten years ago, he and I were hiking through a meadow at the base of a mountain and he was, as he usually is, remote and silent. The sky perched so high above us—no clouds, a few birds diving and swooping. His terrier bounded after a rodent, hindquarters quivering. I asked him, "Do you miss your mother?"

The question was hard to ask. But I realized that if he dropped dead that day, I would not be able to tell anyone a single thing that went on in his head. So I wanted to find out if he had a set of feelings, if he experienced a kind of longing. After all, he'd just lived through something terrible. His mother died in a bathroom, wailing in pain, covered with blood and bile.

"No," my father said and started walking faster. The high grass whizzed by as I hustled to keep up. "I spent my life trying to get away from her." When he said this, something happened with his shoulders, like brine in his chest rose up, turning all his parts turgid. Even his small ears were stiff.

Musical Interlude #1

At this point, I'd like the page to burst into song, but pages don't do that. So instead, imagine that you are a very small child. You are warm and drowsy in the bed you remember, the first bed you ever had. The covers smell like detergent and your pajamas twist uncomfortably under your

arms. Your mother sits next to you and she sings in a war-
bling voice. She doesn't know all the words to the song that
she sings but your body fills with the peace of the noise, the
way her voice is like the fur behind the cat's ears: velvety.
You put your fingers on her thigh and the sounds go round
and round in their haunting way until she switches off the
lamp. Then you are in darkness—that world with its mon-
sters and devil men, and you feel something you can't yet
name—how dangerous it is to be small. So you reach out
and put your tiny perfect hand on the thigh of a woman
whose voice is imperfect and that is the thing you have
holding you here, and it holds you.

My father's hanky-panky, if I can still call it that now that
my mother is dead, began years before she died. I press on
my eyelids and see the white jiggling dots there. I like to
imagine that these dots have power, that they're tunnels to
God. I picture my grandmother's face etched onto one of
them, Ariella's on another. *Go,* I say to the dots. But they
don't know their own power and the lights dissolve into
patterns of gray.

"I need to speak to my son," my grandmother says. "I'm
waiting for his call."

"I heard you," I say.

She opens her purse and takes out a cigarette. With it
clasped between two fingers, she reaches under her slip to
scratch her thigh. Her legs are blue and purple, textured as
the skin of old nectarines.

"Why do you always come here? Why don't you just go visit him?" I ask. She squints and lowers the bottom of her jaw so that her cheekbones look more severe.

"You were an ungrateful child," she says. "You're still that way."

The fact is—though the fact comes at the end of a long story about pogroms, immigration, and the Great Depression— I have this woman's money, the money she and my grandfather saved for decades and that he never allowed her to spend. My grandparents lived in a run-down Brooklyn tenement full of mirrored tables, ceramic figurines, and silver-bound prayer books. It smelled of cooking oil and bleach and in the bathroom my grandmother kept beautiful soap in vivid colors that no one was allowed to use. My grandfather wouldn't permit her to buy a house. He wanted the money—the papery truth of it. A house could burn down. A roof could wear through. A yard would need tending. These things would take a stack of bills and make it smaller and smaller until he was nothing again, just a boy with a father who wandered the streets drunk, muttering to himself in Yiddish.

I spent this money the moment I got the check. I went out, found an extremely small house in this city—a house with a bad roof and a yard with weeds—and bought it. And now we stand in it together, my grandmother and I.

"I don't think that's fair," I say. She takes another drag of her cigarette but there's no smoke, no ember. It's just a prop. The dead can't smoke.

"Do you know all the things I gave up?" she says. "Do you know how life was before it was yours?"

The phone rings. She reaches for it and I reach for it and our hands touch. Her fingers are cold and damp, like sandwich meat. I shrink back and she claws at the receiver.

"Hello?" she screams. How her face expands, those pink lips opening. Her dentures are slightly crooked in a face that could be nineteen years old. And then she's on the ceiling, her breasts hanging toward me like the rungs on the subway and she has the phone smashed against her face and I see she's crying. *"Hello,"* she says again and she dissolves through the roof and the receiver lands with a thud on the wood floor.

Beyond immediate kin, I barely knew my family. My father moved us to Washington State as soon as he finished school. Everyone else lived in Brooklyn. If you held a gun to my head and told me to recite the names of my grandmother's eight sisters, the sisters that meant everything to her, I wouldn't be able to. They're gone and lost, irrelevant.

There's no one on the phone and I set it back in the cradle. I sit down at my desk and check e-mail. My coffee's gone cold. I should clean the house before my father shows up.

Then she's back, this time wearing a poncho.

"You thought you were rid of me," she says. There's a sofa next to my computer table and she sits on it primly. She has the slip on under her poncho and I can see the skeletal outline of her knee joint. "That happens sometimes, that floating." She takes out another cigarette and sticks it in her mouth. "You should have children," she says, the cigarette clamped between her lips. "I thought you were listening when I told you that."

"I'm not too old yet," I say.

My grandmother checks her lipstick in the reflection of a silver lighter. "Your mother was too ambitious," she says. "I never did like her."

And then my mother appears in a Catholic schoolgirl outfit, though she's neither Catholic nor a girl—she is about the age she was when she died: forty-eight. She too has opaque pink lipstick and blue eye shadow. There must be a paucity of good makeup in their world.

"Mom." I reach toward her. But she doesn't acknowledge me.

"Eve," she says to my grandmother. "You're a cunt." My grandmother slowly crosses one leg over the other and I can see she has a bruise the size of my hand on the back of her calf. Her tulip diamonds glitter vehemently in the afternoon sun.

"Extraordinary," says my grandmother, raising her brows.

My mother shakes her head.

"Look at my son," my grandmother says. "He hasn't been happy in as long as I can remember. See what you did to him?"

"Did to him? What did I do?" my mother snaps. "I married him. I had his child. I worked like a dog. What do you want from me?"

"You worked like a dog on that career of yours—as if he couldn't support you, as if his hard-earned money wasn't good enough," my grandmother says. "What was he supposed to do? You got fat like a cow. You were always too busy. So he did what any man would have."

"God," my mother says, smashing her fists into her hips. I can see a roll of cellulite where the short skirt ends.

"You live in a little dark hole, Eve. All his life he was running from *you*."

"Mom," I say to her. She glances over at me and for a moment there it is, the warmth and recognition, but she turns quickly back to my grandmother.

"If you think that when he dies he'll come running back to you, you're an idiot."

My grandmother's chin rises up toward her nose. "When he gets here," my grandmother says, "I've found him a new girl from Queens."

"You're too late," I say and for a moment, my mother turns silver.

And then my grandfather falls onto the couch next to my grandmother, smiling wildly, his head fuzzed with gray curls. He reaches for her sagging breasts, puckering his mouth like he's going to suckle.

"Get away from me," she screams at him. And he does; he's gone in a flash.

"Please go," I say to my grandmother.

"Tss," my grandmother says to my mother. Her eyes are metal now, ready for a fight. "And look at this daughter of yours. With these same ridiculous ideas."

"There's nothing wrong with my daughter," my mother says. "She's beautiful and talented."

"Your daughter," my grandmother says, "is spoiled. A writer, she wants to be, as if God gave her some precious little song that only she can sing."

I leave them then, to go outside and look through the mail.

When I return, my mother is sitting on the sofa. She's taken a wineglass down from the cabinet and sips from it, though it's empty.

"That was draining," she says. "That woman's like a nasal drip. You can ignore her for a while and then—wham—she's too much."

"Mom," I say to her and my eyes get hot, my throat clamps. She looks surprised by this and carefully sets the glass down on the floor. And disappears.

Musical Interlude #2

Another urge for song. Maybe it's that I'm telling this story on a bright day and it has been a rainy, terrible winter. Now the sun is out and I have this mothering desire to put my hand on your hair and pet it, and this time I would sing you an upbeat number. Imagine you are in the car. It's hot. A heat wave and it's the 1970s and the car's seats are beige vinyl. You're alone in the backseat because you, for the purposes of my story, are an only child. So you are pretty much always alone back there and to keep yourself entertained you store small objects in the little pocket behind the driver's seat where other families keep road atlases. In here you have an agate, a toy mouse missing some fur, a coin from Africa, a snail shell with pink inside of it, a doll bonnet, and a plastic giraffe. Your parents are filling the two seats up front. They are both still alive and locked into their routine of arguing.

"I *said* turn right all the way back on Sixth," your mother says. "But you don't listen." She reaches over his lap and presses the turn signal as he turns. "And you never use your blinker. Someday you are going to kill us all." To which your father says, "Stop your self-righteous wankering." And she says, "Wankering? What kind of word is wankering?"

You take out the agate and look at it and you think it's like the eye of your dog, Moose, before Moose died. Then your mother turns to you over the front seat with her long thick braid and those pretty strands that fell over her forehead, sometimes getting caught in the hinge in her big glasses, and she says, "Hi, baby, what are you doing." She never asks you questions, she simply says the question like she's announcing something. She holds out her palm and so you reach into the pocket of the car and grab the giraffe and set it there.

She studies this little plastic animal and then she turns back to look out the windshield of the car, to see the day flashing in, this one day, driving to a softball game or a picnic or something that no longer matters but mattered right then. There is a huge weeping willow tree and a sloping lawn and some dogs running on a hill. All of this falls through the windshield and lands for a moment on the dash and she holds the giraffe and then she starts to sing.

Can you even imagine how young she was then? Listen to her voice, reedy but sweet. It's a song you haven't heard since—some strange song about the foam of the ocean—she probably made it up. And your father pulls over and says, "I don't know where the fuck this is, Nan. Where the fuck is this?" And you wish you could say, for the purposes of the story, that she rolled down the window and sang her song to the passersby, unbraided her hair and shook it around. You want to say that she got out of that car and flung her arms, wildly singing about foam, but actually she just said, "Why don't you look at the *map*?" Then she threw the giraffe back at you and it landed in your lap and she went searching for a map in the glove box.

My father hasn't mentioned my mother in the three years since she died. If I mention her, his face grows still, his nostrils tighten, but he says very little. Maybe: "It's very sad." Maybe: "Life's not fair and no one said it was," but her name, Nancy, doesn't come up. He doesn't hold her sweaters to his face and cry.

Ariella. What can I tell you about this newest choice? In junior high she was sporty. She had thick brown hair and equally thick legs. She smiled with her whole body, like a well-treated dog. With me, he's distant and disinterested. But I'm sure she brings out his charming side.

I start to straighten the house. In my bedroom, I check to see if I've left any dishes and find my grandfather sitting up in bed, mashing Saltines around in his mouth—and since he is dead and can't swallow, spitting the mush into a water glass.

"HELLO HELLO!" he shrieks. Death has not improved his hearing and so he delivers his words at the highest decibel and pitch. "HAVE YOU SEEN YOUR FATHER?" My father still lives about an hour from here, in my childhood home, the home he shared with my mother for nineteen years. I, on the other hand, have moved from place to place. And yet they have no trouble finding their way in here, and none of them seem able to figure out where he is.

"He's home, I think," I say. "But he's visiting later." My grandfather takes out his teeth and wipes them off on the edge of my sheet. He reinserts them and raises his top lip. "These damn things don't fit right anymore," he mutters.

"What do you need?" I ask.

"WHAT?" he screams.

"WHAT DO YOU NEED?" I scream back.

"I DON'T NEED ANYTHING. WHAT DO YOU NEED?"

"I'M TRYING TO CLEAN THE HOUSE," I scream.

"GOOD IDEA," he screams. I stand there looking at him and a gooey hunk of gray cracker slides from his lip into the glass. His eyes are so tiny, like the buttons of a lady's blouse. The skin on his face looks oniony, translucent, and large splotches of gray mottle the greenish hue. He scrunches his face like someone is grabbing his ear and it hurts.

"HE'S COMING FOR A VISIT?" my grandfather says. I nod, then take the crackers off the nightstand and grab the glass. My grandfather doesn't seem to notice. I walk the stuff back into the kitchen, dump the cracker goo down the drain, flick on the disposal, and listen to the grind. With great care, I load the dishwasher. Then I go back into my bedroom.

"HE HAS A NEW GIRLFRIEND," I say. My grandfather turns and looks out the window. The yard is dead. I'm terrible with plants. Even the weeds have turned brown. But there, in the center of a patch of dry, cracked earth, where a better person would have a lawn, my grandmother stands, fooling with the belt of her raincoat.

"THAT'S WHAT I HEAR," my grandfather says. "A SHIKSA. I'D LIKE TO KNOW HOW HE MANAGES."

"HOW HE MANAGES WHAT?"

"HOW HE *GETS ALONG*!" my grandfather wails.

"HOW HE HANDLES HIS MASCULINE NEEDS!"
He's furious now, quivering in the bed, his gray spots turning lavender.

My grandmother appears by the dresser.

"Masculine needs?" she says. Her face is old again,
wrinkled, and her hair is red.

My grandfather tries to respond, but there's too much
saliva in his mouth. He gasps and says through the wet,
"Why do you hate me, Eve?"

"Look at you," my grandmother says, and though she
isn't screaming, my grandfather seems to hear her. "When
I was alive," she says to me, "the best meals I ever ate, I had
to eat with the ladies from the secretary pool because he
wouldn't spend the money."

"WE HAD NO CHOICE!" he wails. "WE HAD TO
THINK OF THE FUTURE!"

"This is the future," my grandmother says. "This is it."

"You should have asked," my grandfather says.

"Ha," says my grandmother. Her mouth is tight. "Get
out of bed." He obeys. Then they are gone.

Though I wasn't there to see it, the legend goes that while
my grandmother was bleeding on the floor of their apartment, my grandfather kneeled in the blood and cried. He
told her how much he loved her and she looked at him and
she looked at him. My grandfather thought she was inca-
pable of speaking, he thought she was being carried off by
God, but she was just listening to him blubber. Finally, she
raised a hand to her forehead, leaving a smear of red, and
said, "Louis, you wouldn't know love if it hit you in the
head." Then she died.

* * *

Back in the living room, there's a disturbing situation. Someone has cut cardboard boxes into little headstones. In black marker, one says Eve, the other, Louis.

"In here, sweetheart!" my mother calls. She's in the bathtub, her head resting against the blow-up pillow. There's no water in the tub and she's still in her skirt, though now she's wearing thick stockings underneath it. "I hope that stuff's not bothering you. I'm trying something to see if I can keep her away."

"The headstones?" I ask her.

"Has Eve ever told you that she hates her monument?" my mother says. "She thinks we were cheap. She thinks she should have had the higher-grade marble, not granite. I told her the marble isn't strong—it wears away so that in fifty years your name is just a smear of lichen, but she doesn't believe me. She says that I convinced your father to buy her a headstone from China."

"We did buy her a headstone from China," I say.

"Well, it wasn't cheap," my mother says.

"So what's with the cut-outs?" I ask her. She sits up in the tub and smooths the skirt down.

"She won't want to be reminded," my mother says. "So maybe she'll stay away."

"Why are you here?" I ask her. Her face gets concerned, the way it did when I was little and told her that I skinned my knee on the driveway.

"You wanted me here."

"I know," I say. "I did."

My mother glances toward her hips. "You need to clean this tub," she says.

Musical Interlude #3

This time, the song is a sad one. You're twenty-four years old and you and your mother sit on a grassy overlook, the Pacific Ocean thrashing beneath you. You're both pretending that it's a much nicer day than it is—pretending that wide, blue skies stretch above. You don't yet know what all of this will mean, this view of sky and water. You think only that oceans seem calming, attached to a force that can soothe you.

She says, "Hold my hand," and you take it and notice it doesn't feel right; it's too cold and rubbery. You fight the feeling of rage that keeps slipping in from the side with its fishtails and its scampering. The black wheelchair sits crookedly in the grass, and for a moment you worry that you will not be able to get it back to the road. Slowly, as you strategize how you will press the wheelchair hard on one side to turn it, the scampering quiets and in its place you feel a desire to ask something. The question is hard to put into words. It feels like you have to ask it in a foreign tongue, and it sits for a long time inside you.

"Do you believe you'll go anywhere after?" you finally ask. It comes out fast. She sits perfectly still, letting the question absorb, and then she starts to cry. She pulls the oxygen tube out so she doesn't clog it and she looks like a fish without air.

She raises her eyes and her shoulders in a gesture of unknowing. For a long time you sit like that, staring out, not noticing anything different about the jutting rocks covered in barnacles and bird shit or the pattern of dull light on a winter sea. Later you'll wonder if that day was marked by God, tagged somehow, but you don't yet know enough to wonder this.

You feel weary, but you aren't through. "If when you die, you can still visit, will you?" you ask her. Your voice breaks here, and you feel ashamed—because your wish right now is so selfish: you don't want to be left in this world alone.

Her dark eyes are filled with the jaded, exhausted seriousness that will become the only seriousness you will ever really trust. "Of course, sweetheart," she says. "You'd be number one."

Now you both listen to the earth's song, the crush of sand beneath water, the cry of gulls—and that is when you notice that there is something creaky about the bench you're on, that the cry of gulls has reached a strange fervor, that the water doesn't sing, it growls.

*

My mother disappears—as they all do—and for the rest of the afternoon, nothing happens. I toss the headstones. I finish the laundry. My father said he would arrive at around seven and by five, I am exhausted.

I lie down on clean sheets, but my mind races. When my mother was dying, my father left town every weekend. He claimed he had meetings he couldn't miss, conferences it would be professionally irresponsible not to attend. My mother lay on the sofa, a blanket over her swollen feet, and watched animal shows on the television. She nodded when he gave his reasons. I don't know what she knew at the time. I don't know what kind of arrangement they had. But she seemed to understand that her absence would simply be that, an absence, a hole, and that he wouldn't know what to do with it other than plug it.

If I say to him, on my birthday, that I miss her, that every happy occasion just brings with it a blur of pain, he shakes his head.

"You can't live in the past," he says. "You have to move on with your life."

But that's not it. It's not that I'm stuck. They're just not as gone to me as they are to him.

At seven, promptly, the doorbell rings. Ariella looks exactly as I remember her. In fact, she even dresses much as she would have in junior high. She wears a plain white T-shirt that's too big for her and tight faded jeans. Her beige moccasins are not stylish and her bangs hang over her eyes.

"Hi," she says to me and I see trepidation in her face, which I appreciate.

I lean in to hug my father. He smells like leather.

They come into the house and I get out some wine. We talk about their drive. We talk about restaurants. We'll go out to eat, sure. How about Thai food? Or do you prefer something else, Ariella? Italian? My father takes his heavy hand and puts it on Ariella's neck the way he used to put his hand on my neck when I was little and he was playing ventriloquist.

When they finish their wine, I gather the glasses and take them to the kitchen. Eve, Louis, and Nancy are all there, hovering together in the doorway.

"Only a goy would wear those shoes," my grandmother says. "What are they made of, elk?" My mother stands soberly beside her.

"She's so young," my mother says, and bites the inside of her cheek. My grandmother gets her rain cap out of her coat pocket and shakes it vigorously.

"Elk," my grandmother says again. "Hmph." My grandfather hovers by her side looking gleeful, his wet mouth twitching.

Musical Interlude #4

My father didn't sing to me. He has no sense of tone, no patience for lyrics. The night she died, he came up to my childhood room, where I'd been staying. I was still awake, my fear gnawing at me, a caffeine of nerves, but I knew he was coming to deliver bad news and so I feigned sleep.

"Hey," he said, knocking quietly on the door frame. I didn't respond. In that silence, a hundred songs, a thousand songs, so many songs that the noise became silence.

"She's gone."

From the sofa, Ariella lets out a high-pitched giggle.

I walk back into the living room and ask them if they're ready to go. Ariella is flushed. My dad grins.

"We're ready," Ariella says, pushing my father's hand off her neck.

I pull my coat from the closet and follow my father and Ariella outside. He opens the car door for her and I breathe in the late-fall air. There will be rain. The air smells like rocks.

"How about Italian, actually," Ariella says, and I can

hear my grandmother saying, "The last thing that girl needs is pasta."

"Italian's fine," I say, climbing into the backseat. "There's a new restaurant just out of town." I glance back at the house. Through the big window, my mother watches us. She makes a shooing motion with her hand. My grandmother snaps her rain cap beneath her chin and adjusts the belt on her coat. My grandfather looks like he's shrinking, but his fists are balled in an approximation of victory.

This time, the pocket behind the driver's seat contains an atlas. I slide it out, flip to this city—its streets colored red and blue—and show them how to go.

Acknowledgments

I am indebted to the readers, teachers, and magazine editors who gave their time, support, and advice along the way, especially Michelle Carter, Peter Orner, Bob Glück, Nona Caspers, Kira Poskanzer, Camas Davis, Laura Davis, Amy Payne, Shayna Cohen, Rob Spillman, and Hannah Tinti. For their attempts at cheerleading and assuaging the crazies, thanks to Richard Romm, Martha Walters, and Suzanne Chanti. The MacDowell Colony provided the community and support that allowed me to write "Family Epic." I'm grateful to Maria Massie for her unwavering faith in this book and to Alexis Gargagliano for being such a kind, thoughtful, and thorough editor. And of course, a special thank-you to Don Waters, who has known these stories from their first halting words, and who has seen me grow up along with them.

About the Author

Robin Romm was born and raised in Eugene, Oregon. Her short stories have appeared in a number of publications, including *Tin House, One Story,* and *The Threepenny Review.* She was a 2006 MacDowell Fellow and lives in Berkeley, California.

INJECTIONS OF INSANITY

LORRAINE MACE

Published by Accent Press Ltd 2019
www.accentpress.co.uk

ISBN 9781786156839
eISBN 9781786156822

Printed and bound in Great Britain by Clays Ltd,
Elcograf S.p.A

INJECTIONS OF INSANITY

LORRAINE MACE

Published by Accent Press Ltd 2019
www.accentpress.co.uk

ISBN 9781786156839
eISBN 9781786156822

Printed and bound in Great Britain by Clays Ltd,
Elcograf S.p.A